what are you like

what are you like

SHELLEY DAY

Short Stories

First published in 2019 by Postbox Press,
the literary fiction imprint of Red Squirrel Press
36 Elphinstone Crescent
Biggar
South Lanarkshire
ML12 6GU
www.redsquirrelpress.com

Edited by Colin Will

Front cover artwork by Nicolai Sclater
e: ornamentalconifer@gmail.com

Typesetting and design by Gerry Cambridge
e: gerry.cambridge@btinternet.com

A CIP catalogue record is available from
the British Library.

ISBN: 978 1 910437 73 5

Red Squirrel Press/Postbox Press are committed
to a sustainable future. This book is printed in
the UK by Imprint Digital using Forest Stewardship
Council certified paper.
www.digital.imprint.co.uk

For my sister, Karin Bao

'It is too late to turn back. Having read the opening words of this book you have already begun to enter the unsettling experience of finding yourself becoming a subject whom you have not yet met, but nonetheless recognise. The reader of this book must create a voice with which to speak (think) the words (thoughts) comprising it... You, the reader, must allow me to occupy your thoughts, your mind, since I have no voice with which to speak other than yours. If you are to read this book, you must allow yourself to think my thoughts while I must allow myself to become your thoughts and in that moment neither of us will be able to lay claim to the thought as our own exclusive creation.'

—Thomas Ogden, *Subjects of Analysis*

'In a poem, one line may hide another line,
As at a crossing, one train may hide another train.
That is, if you are waiting to cross
The tracks, wait to do it for one moment at
Least after the first train is gone. And so when you read
Wait until you have read the next line —
Then it is safe to go on reading. ...'

—Kenneth Koch, 'One Train May Hide Another'

'If we look at our lives we shall probably find that we spend most of our time neither in behaviour nor in contemplation, but somewhere else. I ask: where?'

—Donald W Winnicott 'The Place Where we Live,'
Playing and Reality

* CONTENTS *

Your mother, leaning up at the table in the yard, cleans herring. She calls it cleaning but what she's doing is slitting the fish, throat to anus, hooking out the guts with a single slide of her quick thumb. Pearly purple innards slither into the white enamel pail. Every dozen or so she pushes stray hairs back from her forehead with the inside of her wrist, picks up the sharpening steel and slices the gutting knife criss slick criss slick down alternate rasping sides.

That knife'll have her fingers off, your father throws out over his shoulder as the back-lane door bangs shut behind him.

The air is filled with the stink of herring guts. Silver bodies are piling up, drip dripping bluey bloody watery juice.

The pile begins to slip and slide and your mother picks up the filleting knife and criss slick criss slick criss slick, she tops and tails into a different pail, cracks out backbones, spreads pink grey slivering flesh into butterflies.

The smaller fillets for baking are passed to you. You have to scrape away the scales in the wrong direction. You have to scrape and scrape with your own little knife until no more scales come off. Then rinse rinse rinse in the blue pail. Then salt them and roll them and line them up side-by-side in the thick foil trays, fins up, tidy. A sprinkle of vinegar.

You'll have silver scales stuck to your hands, your arms, your chin, and in your hair. You'll scrub and scrub till you're raw red but some will stay, they always stay. Your mother laughs and says they look for all the world like sequins. She ruffles your hair with her herring hand.

* PICNICKING WITH MY FATHER *

In the night the smell of engine oil, my father come to fetch me. *Howway wor lass, it's time to come.* His voice, soft as the dark, cradles my head like a pillow; the rough stubble of his chin prickles my cheek as he bends over and scoops me up; the sweet oniony smell of sweat on my father's shirt; the soft thud thud thud of his heart. I'm limp, the Lady of Shalott, pale hair, pale limbs, trailing. My father will take me to the river, which is where he comes from and where I like to go.

My teacher will say: Does anyone know the Ouseburn? Hands up.

And I'll say, Yes, me, I do! My father takes me there. For picnics.

Liar! Myra chips in. She's a liar, her. Her dad's in jail. He doesn't even take her nowhere.

But what does Myra know? It had been easier to let them think he'd gone to prison. Whatever. They'll think what they like, regardless.

What my mother says is: good bloody riddance and haven't I even got the sense I was born with. Grandma Ruby can't be doing with palaver and anyway it's Wednesday; I should be holding my tongue and cleaning out the grate.

I clean out the grate on Wednesdays because that's the day my grandma's Ladies come round for the Sitting. Jenny Bingham isn't allowed to touch a thing on Wednesdays, only me. I dust across the lid on the piano and open it. I lift the geraniums down one by one from the little table in the bay window; I squeeze a leaf between thumb and forefinger, sniff the peppery smell. I pull the little card table into the middle of the room taking care not to ruck the carpet. I put on the clean white cloth and smooth it with the flats of my hands. Then the board and the glass and the three candles, and the five chairs around. It's five this week so a bit cramped on one side with two. Finally I clean out the grate and set the fire and at seven pm precisely the Ladies will arrive and my grandma will put a match to the kindling and woe betide if I haven't put enough newspaper.

The Ladies will nod at each other. They'll take off their coats but leave their hats on and keep their hand-bags close to. My grandma at the piano, they'll have a little sing with thin voices before they pull on the white cotton gloves and get started.

Afterwards it'll be candles out and lights on and tea in the primrose cups. After they've gone, there'll be a lingering smell of lavender water and mothballs. And in the morning the sweet dark smell of soot.

My mother says: what a load of old baloney and hasn't she got better things to do.

I won't be doing the grate this Wednesday though. I'll be down by the river, skimming stones, doing cartwheels, picking monkey flowers. Picnicking with my father.

My father always sits on the bank and smokes his pipe while I look about the place and gather things. He lifts his chin up to suck smoke in then glides it out and goes pup pup pup like a guppy only more lop-sided. He can be happy like that for hours. I have plenty of time for doing anything. I could wander off and sometimes do, but never far. There's no point; there's everything I could ever want, right here by the river.

You'd be amazed at the things the old river throws up: mangled bits of metal, chipped green bottles half stuffed with mud, pieces of china, spikes of coloured tin. My favourite: Balls that would have been other children's, bashed in and half-deflated, faded rubber cracked and perished, but still floating. Really that's what makes things special: all those imperfections. You can't help but wonder about the lives those things have led.

They find me down by the river in my flannenette nightie.

My sewing teacher will say: Excuse me, Stella Moon, I think you'll find it's flannelette.

And I'll say to Miss, I'm sorry, Miss.

But I won't mend my ways. I've no intention of mending my ways. Miss imagines that I stand corrected.

They find me at the river's edge with the flannenette nightie that reaches to the ground. They scurry over. They say I am Wee Willy Winkie except I am stood there shuddering with cold. Mud has squeezed up between my toes and dried crusts on the tops of my feet. I watch them mouthing Hush Child and I hear the hiss of whispers; they say I'll have caught my death.

My father has already disappeared. He knows when he's not welcome. He has to go before they come because he's not approved of and neither is the Ouseburn river which is dirty with rats and typhoid and leeches. All my father leaves behind is the smell of engine oil down by the viaduct, down by where the lead-works and the lime-kiln and the pottery used to be, and the great black barges carrying coals from Tynemouth.

Even my grandmother's Ladies don't want my father, or that's what they say. Sometimes though he's all I can get and then they have to make do because beggars can't be choosers. Anyway, I can't choose my baggage any more than they can, and well they know it. But they'd much rather not have him, they make it quite plain:

We'd really rather not have Stella's father *again*, if anyone else is available. Is there anyone else available? Is there, is there anyone there?

The Ladies concentrate their minds and their energies into the special Prayer of Protection; they breathe slowly and deliberately, their old eyelids flicker almost shut, their old hands in the white cotton gloves splayed open on the table, pinkie touching pinkie, thumb pressed against thumb.

They find me down at the river's edge and they wrap me all up in sheets because it's all they have, or it seems the best thing, I'm not sure which. They carry me so my legs dangle and my feet are suspended above the ground. It's as though I'm hovering, as though I could float away. They bring me back to the house; I'm tilted and jolted as they make their way up the steep back steps where dried-up stalks of rose-bay-willow-herb and long snatches of bramble have died trying to get a hold among rubble and stone. I keep my eyes shut and I feel the ladies flinch when the thorns snag at their stockings and they're wishing they weren't having to carry me.

Well they didn't have to. I could have found my own way back as I've done many times before, gliding back by myself under the moonlight, my little stockinged feet barely brushing the cobbles, dull pale with frost. Unlike those Ladies I wouldn't let my shoes slither on the fine green moss that coats the stone. At the old back door I wouldn't need to fumble and fuss with the fat iron key that objects as soon as it feels the warmth of a hand. It occurs to me as they push at the door with their skinny shoulders just how burdensome their lives are.

The door cracks then creaks open and I'm almost up-righted in the haste and I'm being borne across the wide empty hall. Clack cleck clack clack echoes the army of stout shoes on the polished parquet. Swish switch swish go the thick stiff skirts that waft strict smells of carbolic and starch. Which of these Ladies who touches me with the white cotton gloves is successfully stifling a pall-bearing thought?

I don't open my eyes until they've unravelled my sheets, set me down at the table, and splayed open my hands.

It's mostly dark where you have to go on Wednesdays. They think you don't mind, but you do, and they can't know you do. What they want is what matters, and you go along with it, you go along with it, because there's no other way.

The Ladies exhale the smells of dentures and Rennies. It's not unpleasant, but they forget how sensitive you are, even to these small things. They don't know how thin your skin is, how hardly even visible, stretched as it is over your filigree of vital purple veins, transparent as an unborn child. The Ladies can't know the terrible weight of the longing that seeps out from their fond little mouths, that squeezes between their teeth, from under their soft wet tongues, through their lips drawn back tight and dispelling. They're sucking teeth and mints and swallowing sin and spitting out prayer and they're expecting you to catch it all and carry it all: the weight of words. Well you can't. You can't. With the best will in the world, no-one can.

One day you'll take them down to the ruined Mill. How often down at the Mill you've sat with your father and you've picked armfuls of yellow flag irises and monkey flowers and you've laid them funereal on the bank.

Or you've tucked your skirt into your knicker-legs and you've paddled in, oops, oops, slipping, sliding on stones slime-green with algae, almost but not quite losing your footing, you hold yourself up with wavered outstretching of your arms.

Gan canny, wor Stella, your father whispers, *gan canny, bonny lass*.

You look up. You hadn't known your father was there today, that he was watching. But you're glad of him, and you realize this is what you'd been hoping for, waiting for: whatever else is this sliding silly performance on algae, on stones that cut your feet, in this stinking river milky with death, what else is it all for?

You determine. You will cross. You will cross the river to the other side, to the side where your father waits.

You're very cold but nearly half way there, nearing the middle where there'll be no point in turning back.

Your father is waiting on the other side and man and boy he was by this filthy river and his father before him and his before that, all of them man and boy while the foundries smoked and the glassworks smoked and the flint mill and the flour mill and the flax mill and the molten lead squeezed flat in the rolling mill and the smoke sunk low all around the viaduct and down down around where the little houses crouch in tight together. Man and boy.

For you, now, the Ouseburn is a rubicon of leeches that suck at your ankles, that attach, glutinous, gluttonous, sticking until you can dislodge them with sharpened sticks.

Further in and the opaque grey water gushes round your thighs and it's hard to stay standing even with your feet half-sunk in mud. Your skirt's come out at the back and it's soaked and slapping at your bare wet legs. Behind you the wind makes the thin trees wince and growls hungry at the Mill with its crumbling stone and gaping black windows, empty eyes that watch as you march on, more slowly now, your thigh muscles braced push against the water.

Your father is there, standing on the bank, holding out his hands.

When the river reaches your waist you stretch up your arms into the air, your thin red skirt lashes around you as if trying to escape. Then the river is gripping your chest and for a moment you are a ballet dancer pirouetting pirouetting, catching glimpses of everything all run in together. You hear the wind and the rush of the wild river thrashing. The river tumbles you and tumbles you and then you are floating. Shreds of your red skirt froth in the culvert where you come to rest.

The guide-book says: Once a cradle of industrialisation, the Ouseburn Valley is now a cultural hub, well worth a visit. It has a regeneration trust and some original industrial buildings: Come in and see the photographs. There are riding stables, studios, shops and galleries, and real ale and music to be had every night at The Cluny.

Stella and her father sit together on the river-bank and they laugh and they laugh and they laugh. They say: Look at it, look at the filthy Ouseburn, it refuses to be gentrified. They sit side-by-side under the viaduct and they skim stones across the water and enjoy their picnic.

You find yourself in an Instagram post placed by a stranger you've been following for no reason other than he posts in black and white and always only a solitary subject and from the back.

Alone in a white black-banded hat, below-the-knee-skirted and baseball-booted you follow yourself walking across a white chequered square. You are carrying two bags, one permanent, one transient. Alongside you your shadow curves, its whereabouts, its movement, its rhythm, its pace—its very existence—dependent on light. Your stride is your own, and that delirious swish of your skirt.

I saw my grandpa at the funeral, I tell Grandma Ruby when we're back home and we've had the tea and everybody's gone, all except Mr Fanshaw that is.

Don't you be getting above yourself, Grandma Ruby says.

Baloney, my mam chimes in.

My mam's not supposed to be there but she is. They're doing dishes at the scullery sink, Grandma Ruby washing, my mam Muriel drying. I'm meant to be putting away.

Did so, I say.

Grandma Ruby sloshes the dishwater into the sink and upends the bowl.

Carry on like that and people will think you're away with the pigeons, Muriel says.

She can't stand any of it. She dries the last of the pans and hangs it on its hook.

Well, I did anyway, I say under my breath.

I follow the cat into the back kitchen, his tail straight as a poker.

Mr Fanshaw is sat there by the fire in the chair which is not supposed to be his chair because it's actually my grandpa's chair. He's glued to last week's Football Pink. He's still got his smart coat on, but his hat's beside him on the table.

I saw Grandpa Worthy, I blurt out.

Mr Fanshaw peers over the top of his paper, frowns, then lays a bony finger against the side of his nose and winks. I wish he wouldn't do that.

Come and get these dishes put away, our Stella, Muriel shouts through.

Now in she comes, drying her hands on the tea-towel, giving me the Look. She smiles at Mr Fanshaw as she hangs the wet towel on the string that's draped under the mantelpiece for the purpose, and then she's off upstairs with my grandma to do the beds. They're late getting done today, due to the funeral, and hence Muriel's involvement.

I go through to the scullery and sit on the back step. The cat comes through. I wonder why no-one ever thought to give the cat a name. He could have been called Mouser because he's meant to be a mouser. I lick my finger and rub some scuffs off my new patent leather shoes. The sky is thick and heavy-looking like it could collapse any minute and crush the lot of us. He didn't look like a ghost. You couldn't see right through him for a start. He just looked like he always did with his waistcoat undone and his watch chain hanging out of his pocket. And he was wheezing. The yard door rattles, the latch lifts and Myra puts her head round.

You're back, she says.

Myra heaves her brother's bike through into the yard after her and rests it against her leg so she can lean over and pull the back-lane door to.

I saw my grandpa, I tell her.

Oh, she says, did he have those teeth?

She's heaving the door shut, still hanging onto the bike. She believes me.

I saw that film, Myra says, when they keep on coming out of coffins and like turn into bats, well I think they're bats, and like they've got these great big teeth and sink them into people's necks and suck their blood out when they're asleep. Myra pulls back her lips and bares her incisors. Ginormous teeth.

I don't reply. Myra shrugs. She opens the door again and starts dragging the bike out. She should make up her mind if she's coming or going. She's having trouble getting one leg over the crossbar. Her brother's bike is miles too big. Plus it's a lads' one. She gets half-way on then gets stuck.

Put garlic, she advises, on the window-sill. And round the door. They're scared of garlic.

I said I saw my grandpa, dope, I say, my grandpa's not a vampire.

Well, I don't know then, says Myra. She's managed to get onto the bike. I stand and watch as she goes wobbling off up the back lane, balanced on the cross bar.

S'long Stell, she shouts without looking back.

She never stays long at ours, Myra doesn't; her brother says she says we're weird but she says she never said that and it's him that's weird.

It's starting to sleet. The cat won't like it so I pick him up and carry him in. He digs his claws into my shoulder. I feel his breath at my ear and smell his fluffy damp cat smell. Mr Fanshaw is still sat there in the back kitchen.

Have you actually seen a ghost, Mr Fanshaw? I say, putting the cat down.

He struts off, swishing his tail. Mr Fanshaw takes his glasses off and lays them on the table beside his hat. He folds the football pink in four and stands up to stuff it into his coat pocket. Mr Fanshaw always has this white stuff at the corners of his mouth, like he's starting ectoplasm. Now he's making a big thing of tucking his shirt into his trousers. Then he has the hand in his trouser pocket and he's rattling his change. I look down at his dusty cracked black boots and then at my own shiny new patent leather shoes.

Get away with you, he says, still rattling.

He's going a bit red in the face.

I saw one today, I say. Grandpa Worthy.

Divvent talk daft, yer only a kid, Mr Fanshaw says. Howway over here though, I've got summat better than ghosts.

What's that then?

It's magic, he says. Won it at the Hoppings.

Where's it?

In me pocket, he says. You'll have to get it out. Hurry up though. Before they come back down.

Mr Fanshaw's getting breathless, like my granda did, before he died. I feel quite sorry for Mr Fanshaw. He could die as well and nobody will miss him. My mam Muriel says he's just one of Grandma Ruby's lame dogs.

Finders keepers? I say.

Aye, all yours, he says, but you'll have to be quick about it.

I step towards him. He catches hold of my wrist and pushes my hand down into his trouser pocket and holds it there. There's some kind of creature in there. I try to pull my hand back out but Mr Fanshaw is gripping my wrist too tight.

I don't want it, I say, trying to curl my fingers up. I've changed my mind.

She doesn't want the magic frog? Well that's a pity that's a great pity, he huffs. I'll have to give it to some other kid who'll have the decency to be grateful…

A magic frog? I say, hesitating.

Mr Fanshaw nods, pushes my hand back in.

Afterwards, I remember what Myra said and I take a whole thing of garlic from the pantry and run up to our attic and pull it to bits and lay it in a line along by the window. I put on my silver sparkly Cinderella shoes and my pink lacy tutu and my diamond tiara and I lie down flat on my bed, my legs straight out, eyes shut, arms folded across my chest. I breathe slowly and regularly so my chest hardly moves.

Here comes Ruby and Muriel puffing up the attic stairs with armfuls of sheets and pillow-cases and towels freshly ironed. I know without even opening my eyes because I can smell the ironing.

My mam says, Off the bed our Stella, and she slaps my foot.

And what does she think she's doing in that get-up, I'd like to know, Grandma Ruby says.

I lie there, stock still.

Come on, do what you're told, my mam says, slapping my foot again so my shoe comes off, we want to get that bed done.

I'm asleep, I whisper out of the corner of my mouth, I'm asleep for a hundred years.

My mam sighs. Get off that bed our Stella before I land you one. She sounds too tired to be angry but would be angry if she could muster up the energy. I take a risk and stay put.

I'm waiting for the handsome prince, I say by way of explanation.

I'm keeping my eyes tight shut, I'm trying not to move my mouth.

Well you can wait elsewhere, she says, we've got to get the beds done.

I kissed a magic frog, I say, sitting up. I straighten the tiara, tug at the waistband of the tutu which is actually a bit tight.

Grandma Ruby snorts half a laugh. Would you credit

that girl? she says. And what the devil's she got here? She picks up the bits of garlic and stuffs them into her apron pocket. She looks at me and shakes her head. I'm telling you, she's a walking story book, that one.

God only knows what she'll think of next, Muriel says.

Today, some shackles lifting; when I'm alone, a lighterness of spirit, more like I am occupying myself, instead of being someone pretending to be someone pretending to be me.

I'm out for a walk in the sun in Norway. I like that.

I like that I've left my laptop charging in the van, that it will be ready when I am. I like our van.

I like that this pencil I bought in Paris is worn down and small. Like Ali Smith, I think these things are important. I like Ali Smith.

I like that Andrew has had such a grand time at his Lamda reunion and is looking forward to coming 'home' and getting on with the *gapahuk* except he's not because this is not Home and there's no-one to help so all else will be next year if we live that long.

OMG the beautiful dappled light along this little dusty road.

A photograph please from my favourite spot on this lovely warm day.

I feel safe when I take photographs, when I carry these things in my Fjällräven backpack. Do not judge me. I'm not a person who finds it easy to feel safe. There are reasons. Reasons you don't know and I don't care to explain.

The sun now is coming down hot. Two young women pass by carrying water. People in Norway walk to enjoy with serious intent. I'm a stroller. A flâneuse. I was born a city girl. I have had to taste a different life.

I stop at the *bom* where the track begins to descend.

I turn to go back because I am wearing the wrong

jumper, the black 'Cheers' one that is too warm for how hot it's suddenly become and my drink bottle is finished and I don't like the downward trend. I like to think I could plan things, come out equipped and not have to turn around. But hey. Every even small outing in this place lifts the spirits and is good for the soul.

I like how comfortably my Blundstone boots go on, my sand-shoes fit, my days my own.

Grandad Parker, sitting in his wingback chair, rasps his breath, bare veiny feet in misshapen corduroy slippers rest on the brown tiled hearth. The fire cracks and sputters. My grandmother, in her paisley wrap-around housecoat, comes in and dusts the mantelpiece; she lifts the ornaments one by one, rubs them with the yellow duster, and puts them back. She's already done the brasses.

She says, They've given we those blummen cheap coals again. And He shouldn't be sitting up so close to that fire. There's ney telling some folk. He'll kna' aboot it when a spark lands. My grandmother shakes her head like she always shakes her head then she rattles the last of the coals onto the fire and goes out taking the empty scuttle with her. Thick brown smoke hisses up the chimney through a layer of powdery black slack.

In the room—it's not the front room or the living room, it's just the room—the smell of coal smoke, brass polish, laundry. Mist on the insides of the windows; outside, rain. The back kitchen door is open; the boiler gulps out great clouds of steam as my grandmother lifts the lid with a folded teatowel and, leaning back, prods at the contents with wooden tongs held the full length of her arm.

Cara and me, in matching shorts—hers blue, mine green—kneel up at the table. We have little press-studded packs of Lakeland crayons—the pouches smell of custard. We like the rain because we have jotter pads, colouring books, magic painting, thin thin paintbrushes, water in an egg-cup shaped like a shoe.

My grandfather sits watching us. He says, Howway bonnie lass, pass us me coupon over, help us fill it in.

It's time to do the Pools, win some money. I have to fill the coupon in because Nanna doesn't live in cloud-cuckoo land, you daren't ask our Derek, and my sister doesn't know the first thing.

I've finished my magic painting anyway. I hold it up to look, blow on it, shake it a bit to make it dry. It's a donkey, standing in a field with some daffodils that have come out brown. The paper's gone lumpy with the wet. I kneel up and sing a wee song we learned at school: *Daffodil shiny peep through the green, prettier lady never was seen* ... Cara, looking up at my picture, sucks at the bristles on the end of her paintbrush, there's blue all round her mouth.

My grandad leans forward, lifts his arm and prods his bent finger in the direction of the football coupon. He says that finger came from the war but Nanna says what rot, he never went near any blinking war.

Howway bonny lass... My grandad starts, but his words dissolve into coughing. He rests one hand on the mantelpiece and the other on his knee and he coughs and he coughs till he retches up with it then he spits into the fire and wipes his mouth on his hanky. I lay my picture down carefully away from my sister and stand on my chair to reach the *Vernon's* from off the top of the china cabinet. My nanna puts her head round the door and looks at my grandad then at me. I'm not supposed to get him agitated.

Mind ye divvent fall, is all she says before she shakes her head and disappears into the back kitchen.

My grandad is just wheezing now, getting his breath. His fingers scrabble in his cardy pocket, feeling for the biro.

The best thing my grandad likes is his football pools. I get to fill it in with tiny little crosses in tiny little squares. He says you can tell I won the prize for neat writing (I had to copy out 'This Royal Throne of Kings' in actual ink). You have to be exact and you don't get a second chance. That's what my grandad tells me: in all the important things, there are No Second Chances. He says, now mind you remember that, bonnie lass.

If you win the pools you get loads of money. Enough to buy Nanna a holiday and me a typewriter. I'd printed an entire story with the *John Bull* our Derek got me up at Brand's and it took forever and then Grandad said, The lassie needs a typewriter, that's what she needs. We saw a child's one, a Lilliput, in Sheena Robson's catalogue but it was too much. Unless, my grandad said, unless we win the pools, and he tapped the side of his nose with his war finger and winked. Nanna was sitting in the other chair, darning. She wound the strand of wool round her finger and snapped it, then she looked up and shook her head. Then she put her work away in the basket and got up to do the teas.

That day I filled out the pools coupon double quick because Davy next door came knocking for the money so I was dreading in case I hadn't done it right. On Saturday I wasn't there for the checking because I was away up the Gull Ponds with Rosemary Patterson. We'd come back late because we'd seen a dead sheep floating in the rushes, its belly all swollen and its legs sticking up stiff in the air and the smell of it had knocked us sick. When I came flying in the door my nanna was there in the back kitchen. She said, hey, steady on now, and went on prodding at stock which happened to be a sheep's head boiling with peelings and barley and I felt even sicker at the sight of it and I said I'm going to be sick. Get away with you, my nanna said, laughing. Then she said, Your grandad's won the pools, and kept on stirring at the stock. Go on, she said, go and ask him, and she laughed some more.

I clean forgot about the sick and the dead sheep because I was so excited. I ran straight next door to get Sheena Robson's Grafton's. She couldn't believe it and had to come into ours to verify while Davy washed his hands from cleaning out the ferrets and came in too. A typewriter was ordered and Mrs R said you can pay it off week by week but there'll be no need for that in this case, will there, and she laughed and ruffled my hair and called me Little Miss Lucky.

When the typewriter came I got all in a muddle trying to open the box without taking the string off and Nanna said, Goodness sake girl, have patience, and she went to get the scissors. I wound in the special typewriting paper our Derek had brought from up the street and then I had to decide whether to flick onto the black or the red. I couldn't make my mind up so I had a go with both: I wrote 'the quick brown fox jumps over the lazy dog' in both colours and then in capitals and my grandad said, Hey steady on lassie or your ribbon'll be finished before you've even started, and I put my arms around his neck and said he was the best grandad even if he did have no teeth and smelt of remedies and he said not to talk so daft.

My typewriter had a special case that required some careful manoeuvring to get the lid back on and at first I got cross with it and tried to force it and Grandad stood up and said, No no no lassie, that's not the way to do it. And he made me laugh even though I was cross because he said it in a funny gratey voice that sounded like Punch and Judy. He came to where I was kneeling on the carpet and he helped me get the lid on and that was the strangest thing because my grandfather never got up off his chair and he certainly wasn't supposed to walk across the floor. He had to get back double quick because we heard Nanna coming down the stairs with the hot water bottles and she looked worried when she saw him out of breath for no apparent reason.

That first day I typed up a poem about my dog I'd written specially. Grandad said it was champion and wor little Sadie would be writing books one day, and he slapped his leg as if he couldn't quite believe what he'd just said. I made a lovely pattern round the edge and coloured it in with the Lakelands and wrote underneath in fancy writing To the bestest granda and Nanna said there's no such word. But she hung it up on the wall anyway. She hung it next to Grandad's little water-colour of the mill down by the Ouseburn that he painted from memory from when he was a lad, from before he got sick through breathing in the industry that sunk down there, down under the viaduct and around the little cottages where he was born.

Not long after I got my Lilliput, my grandfather died peacefully in his sleep, it was said. I wondered how anyone would know. Oh, they know, my nanna said, shaking her head, they know alright.

One day, a few weeks later, Mrs Robson came round but Nanna was out cleaning. I was by myself and I asked politely, What can I do for you Mrs Robson? She said, Oh I've only just come for the typewriter money, but if your nanna's not here, well... I asked her how much it was. A shilling, she said, for this month, and the same for last. I gave her a two-shilling piece out of the coal money and she said, Well that's all fettled then, a big weight off my mind. When Nanna came in I didn't know what to say. I had to tell her something though because the coal man would come on Monday and she'd be short and there'd be ructions. She was cross and said whatever was I thinking of and money doesn't grow on trees. I said, but I thought my grandad won the pools, and my nanna said, Well it just goes to show, doesn't it, you're not paid to think, and when I want you to think, I'll let you know.

Grandad Parker dies when Sadie is nine. See her, sitting there, half-way up the stairs, pressing her skinny shoulder against the banister 'til it hurts. Ladies in bristly black coats that stink of mothballs file by and go To Look.

See Sadie's little sister Cara sneak in among the skirts of the dark trooping ladies. When she's discovered, Cara screams, clutches onto the bedside table and won't let go.

Sadie's in Trouble for not keeping an eye on Our Cara and for not having the sense she was born with.

Later, Sadie asks her sister what death looks like. Cara shrugs and says she doesn't know; she's only gone in to get Grandad's sweets from off the bedside table. She hands Sadie the crumpled poke to count out half.

Safe under the bed-covers Sadie and Cara peel half-stuck-on papers off the Fox's Glacier Mints and suck themselves to sleep.

* THE SHOES *

Late summer in 1964 and Sadie's mother is taking her to the Stores in Newgate Street to get The Uniform. The Letter says Very Pleased to inform you Sadie Emmeline Geneviève Parker has Passed for the Grammar and she has to get the Uniform and a list is enclosed for your Convenience please to tick the items off. What the whole thing means, Sadie hasn't the foggiest. Her mother says *bloody good job as well* but wishes out loud that Sadie had never been born. And how can it be a good job when Myra's going to Middle Street and Janis'll be stuck down at Chilly Road.

Sadie and her mother get off the bus before the corner and there's the Stores across the way, a massive great grey clout of a building that comes from the Iron Curtain according to Mrs Pinchbeck.

Sadie's mother is pulling Sadie over the road by the wrist. She has on her lets-get-it-over-with look. Sadie can tell from the back of her head, the taut of her arm, the tight of her grip; she can't see her mother's face, but she knows her teeth are clamped together, her thin lips barely showing. Sadie lets herself be pulled along.

Sadie's mother's hair is badly done. The hair closest to her scalp is brown and straight, but the ends are blond and frizzed from the 'Toni' she did last month. Sadie looks down at her mother's feet and sees how she leans over on the insides of her shoes; they're worn down lopsided and have gone all bulgy. Sadie's mother needs new shoes more than Sadie does. Sadie looks at her own feet, treads each step exactly where her mother's has been. She adjusts her style of walking, putting the heel down first, toes last, and bending the arch in the middle. She puts one foot dead in front of the other and doesn't go over on the sides, no way.

It's hot in the Stores, Sadie is fit to roast, but taking off the good coat is not an option. Her mother is heading for the shoe department. Sadie hates and detests the shoes in here. They're old-fashioned, little kids' shoes and she's not a little kid any more so why do they have to come in here why can't they go to a proper shop why can't they go to Isaac Walton's like Andrea Pallister.

Sadie's mother is acting all positive to the sales lady; she doesn't want a scene. She'll put on her posh voice in a minute. She's already smiling in that way she only ever does in shops; she thinks she's being dignified, but to Sadie it's a don't-you-dare-open-your-mouth sort of smile. She feels it in the grip of her hand, senses it in the way her mother won't look at her eyes.

Now Sadie's mother is picking up a shoe from the shelf, it's a horrible lace-up thing, brown leather, snub-nosed. Sadie's has this kind since she was about six, these are not much different, they've tried to update the style with stupid patterns all round where the laces go, they're even more hideous than the plain kind. Inside it says Start-Rite and there's a picture of two children, hand in hand, back view. That means it's a good make. Classy. They're good for your feet. Sadie knows all that. Plus they're the most expensive kind. But surely it's mad to spend all that money when you haven't even paid the rent. But that's not an issue this time. Sadie realises her mother can pay for these because she's taken a Club out, just for The Uniform. Her mother's hand is in her pocket now, feeling for the card, checking again that she hasn't lost it. Sadie will have to try the shoes on.

Please God. Please don't let them have my size.

Sadie is ready to promise God anything. But already the sales lady is coming back; she is smiling, opening the box as she approaches, unfolding the tissue paper, she's taking one out, pulling at the laces to loosen them. She gets down on her knees and uses a shiny shoe horn to fit the shoe on Sadie's foot; she squeezes, checking that it's wide enough, that there's enough room for Sadie's toes, enough room for Sadie to grow. Then she says for Sadie to walk around, and she does, in an exaggerated up-down, one-shoe-off-and-one-shoe-on movement; the lady asks if it's comfy and Sadie looks down and says nothing. Then the lady sits Sadie down again and puts the other shoe on the other foot and laces it up, she's smoothing her hand over the top, then she straightens up, smiles, wipes her hands down the sides of her skirt.

We'll take these, Sadie's mother says, she'll keep them on.

Sadie doesn't want to keep them on but the sales lady is picking up the old shoes and going over to the till and beckoning Sadie's mother to the front of the queue. Now Sadie's mother is too quick to hand over the Club card; she has to keep on holding it there, holding it out, her arm outstretched and vacant, while the sales lady takes too long to pack up the scabby old shoes in the box and wraps them too carefully in the tissue paper. Everyone is looking. Everyone is staring their eyes out. Everyone knows they're getting Sadie's shoes on a Club. Sadie's mother tilts her chin, like the fact of the Grammar is enough for dignity, like it's enough to eclipse even this but it's not and now Sadie too wishes she'd never been born.

* CARRYING ON *
Gudbrandsdalen, Norway, July 2018

My mother is shouting up the stairs, Stop that bloody carry-on. She means something terrible will happen if me and my sister keep carrying on. My sister Cara will verify this as she can verify many things. Cara knows about carrying on.

There was a time when I could no longer carry on and it was my sister who carried me on and this at a time when she herself was broken and black and blue. I crouch in an adjacent room to the noises of black and purple and blue.

In Barter Books I come across postcards, mugs, totes and teeshirts, all pronouncing in red and white, *Keep Calm and Carry On*. It's some good British slogan from World War 2 and, you know, I'm thinking, is this for real? Keep Calm? A massive great big fucking war on and it's Keep Calm? Not always the best instruction, is it. Not always the best thing to do at all

now here's an orange butterfly on a pinky purple blue meadow cranesbill

and frankly sometimes–often–Calm's not an option, like now when you're watching the loom of resurgent fascism, like when you see in conflict zones women raped and raped and girls raped and refugees having to flee and when home is no place to be; no, Calm's not an option when your world's turning upside down for whatever reason or no reason

so many harebells in the hedge here, so blue, and a yarrow

Throw yarrow stalks for the I-Ching to help you decide

what is a good decision and what is not, what might be a good way forward, out of some predicament, or towards some desired goal, personal, political.

The yarrow flower, white, with red ladybirds walking on top isn't here, it's somewhere else; a green grass verge in Brewery Lane by Davy Cox's Milk Bar, the brewery gone even back then, and the Milk Bar sold and sold again and recently all painted up in National Trust colours in the current fad for before. Yarrow can be white or pinkish.

Here growing tall in the shelter of the old furu fence are the tall blue-purple monkshood that stop your heart. Keep calm. Stop your heart. Hold a buttercup under your chin. Does it shine?

Carry on.

Do you like butter? Yes, I think you do. You do like butter, My turn please. See if I do. No me. Let me.

The sound of sheep bells. Two ewes and four fat lambs snatch at young shoots of dwarf birch as they make their way up the road that passes along the forest edge.

The sound of water. You picture a stream, how it comes splashing over the mossy rocks where little blue-purple butterworts cling on at the sides and how the water lashes narrow into the culvert to flow under the road.

Keep Calm. Carry on.

You've had a lot of anxiety lately when your heart beats too fast and you sweat and go cold and feel like you'll pass out and you have to lie down and you tell yourself very sternly Keep Calm.

Mind over matter. Keep calm. Carry on.

You had a boyfriend once called Michael Sterne, in Brewery Lane, when you were eleven. Can people have boyfriends when they are eleven? You did.

Dwarf willow, do you know your leaves are almost

furry, almost silver. You have made your home in the ditch where the damp is. If you land in the ditch, make use of the damp, you'll win out there if the weather stays warm.

The old furu fence slopes and peels its bark in the short hot summers and long cold winters, it weathers what comes and what goes, it does its thing, keeping animals in and out or out and in, enclosing the kve that runs all the way down to the Feforvann, steep and purple-blue with cranesbills and knapweeds, and where have those sheep gone with those clanking bells

where all the people from those bombed places their houses rubbled their hope boats trying to steer the wide sea

Some things carry on over time, echoes of voices from far from calm. Here by the wide lake sounds carry across the water and arrive as full as when they began.

Listen. Late spring. A blue-black cuckoo on the other side makes himself known and known and known again.

Red clover, a bee, and the gate that creaks and the cattle-bridge that rattles. Cross over. Go through. Carry on. Keep calm.

You lose your virginity in the Spinney Flats, you look for it, you call out, you yell; cannit find it anywhere. Johnny, you call, Johnny, Johnny. But nothing happens and it is lost lost lost.

Now the Spinney Flats are right next to the High Heaton Library and across the road from the school. So when you bunk off it's a toss up: the library or the Spinney Flats. You spend your dinner money in the Co-op on the corner—a cheese roll and a bag of crisps. You're not meant to eat stuff in the library but who cares. If it's the canny lass on she'll act like she's not seen nowt.

Nice little irony, you have to admit; kids nicking off school to hang out in the library. You look round the books but only 'cos there's nowt else to do. Some look not too bad though. Dennis Wheatley. A whole shelf on the occult, you'll come back to that. You like the library: the quiet and the space and the rules-all-broken and the freedom of kidding yourself there'll be something else out there, something better than this.

You surprise yourself by pinching one of the library books and you tell yourself that's what people do when they're hungry, so very hungry. *The Face of the Sun King-doms* opens up South America, Peru, the Incas, the Aztecs, ancient stuff, amazing colour pictures of amazing high-up places and that's where you're going, right to the top of that frigging Machu Picchu. The book's got your longings all up and running. Assuming you can hang onto yourself or what bits of yourself you can grab before they float away, you're gonna be headed to South America pronto.

But hey, you're stopped in your tracks when you meet Jack Kerouac half in the library and half in the Spinney flats. Ginsberg and Corso are pissing in the lift, Neal Cassady's sat on the bench outside smoking a joint; he says, man, man, New York's where it's at, man ... OK, OK, New York it is. But then the library chucks Anais Nin in your face and it's her now giving out the orders and it's a houseboat on the Seine and all you can think of is Paris Paris, you're obsessed by Paris and Djuna Barnes and Gertrude Stein and the black cat jumped on her mother's back and hey, imagine, Paris.

Back at base camp and Grandma Ruby's saying, For Christ's sake our Stella put a sock in it. That bloody library filling your idiot head with those stupid ideas, I'll bloody Paris you, she says. ... She goes on and on, your Grandma does. She's not caught up. She's no idea you've got waylaid up the Spinney Flats.

* THE HOLE *

After she spoke, there fell an awkward silence; it came tumbling down from the ceiling and crashed around them on the floor.

He stared at her, his face blank, accusing. He would be unforgiving. As the rubbled silence fell she could tell he was unforgiving to the core. She saw he had a scheme for deciding things, that what she'd said didn't fit. Still she felt responsible.

He wanted her to feel what he felt. Guilt was uppermost in his scheme of things, guilt the cudgel, shame the scalpel he was fingering now in his trouser pocket.

It's a misunderstanding, she wanted to say, I didn't mean what you thought ... what I was trying to say was ... But it was too late. The silence had crashed down around them and they were up to their knees in the rubble of it.

His small eyes shifted to indicate a spade that was propped against a wall. She reached for it and began to shift the rubble. She shifted it into piles like pyramids then she started to dig.

She dug and she dug, she dug a hole in the middle, and the hole was dark and as deep as herself. He never took his eyes off her as she piled the fresh soft earth neatly round the rim of the hole.

She was sweating, the loose sheet wrapped around her stuck to her body with the damp of her sweat. Still she stood tall. It was important to stand tall. She pushed her hair back from her forehead with the inside of her wrist. Her face showed not a trace of anything as he lifted the spade from her hand.

The night before my geography exam I get back to my mam's and find our Cara gone. She's left a note and nicked off with the housekeeping. The note says London.

My mam's away and I'm back supposed to be in charge.

I stuff the note in my pocket and go round to my nan's. She's washing up after the boarders' teas.

Our Cara's gone, I say. Run away.

I hand my nan the note. She takes her pinny off, dries her hands on it, turns the wireless off and fumbles in her cardy pocket for her glasses. We sit down at the table and she reads the note.

My nan phones the police and reports a missing person, a child, she says, barely fifteen.

The police come. They rummage about in Cara's room. I tell them the names of some friends she had at school, and no, there wasn't a boyfriend, not as far as I know. No, I don't think she knows anybody in London, she's never even been there. And no, I don't know why she's gone. They take the note away, and last year's school photograph from off my nan's mantelpiece, and her Cinderella cushion for the sniffer dog.

We wait for phone calls, but none come. My nan rings round some rellos; nobody knows anything, but they're all ears, you can imagine.

The next day I go to school, but my mind's a blank for glaciation and the tundra. I tell Lizzy and she says to go home with her, but in the end I go back to my nan's. Nothing, my nan says when I walk in. No news is good news. Yeah, well, I say.

My nan makes mince and dumplings and I eat mine with Mr Carly from the Electric Board. He's stumped, he says, it's beyond him what kids think they're on about these days. Then he sneaks me one of his Number 6 when my nan's not looking, and I save it in my school bag for after.

The police come round—it's a woman this time—and they say Nothing as yet, but Rest Assured No Stone will be Left Unturned. Then she wants to speak to me, by myself. We go through to the front room, which is normally only used on Sundays and at Christmas. Granda's mantelpiece clock from when he left the pit has a very loud tick. My nan likes to keep it wound up. There's a smell of old soot from the chimney and a peppery scent from the geraniums on the table by the window. The police woman—Mandy, she says, Call me Mandy—sits on the edge of the sofa and flicks through the paperwork resting on her lap.

You've no idea what's behind this then, she says.

I shake my head. I say, No, no idea, no idea at all.

Was your sister…was Cara…was she happy at home, she asks, I mean, she must've had a reason, to go, to go like this, if it's not a, a, a boyfriend thing…

I shrug.

Then Mandy sits up straighter, looks me crisply in the eye and in a different voice she says, Sadie, it's vitally important that you tell us what you know, *everything* you know. If you want your sister found.

They've been to Cara's school—where she used to go that is, she's been left there more than a year.

I shrug again.

Well, my nan says, what did that policewoman want then?

Mandy, I say, she's called Mandy.

Well what did Mandy want then, my nan asks.

My nan says Mandy like it's a disease, like she can't stand having the word in her mouth. My nan can't abide anything that involves people poking their noses into other people's business. She's sitting at her table sticking golden ric-rac braid onto the red felt jacket of a tiny beefeater doll. It's fiddly work. Her fingers aren't what they used to be and she's having trouble getting the braid in place. There's a small pile of dolls already finished and another pile of little red hats waiting ready to go on.

Shall I do the hats, I say.

But my nan doesn't answer. I didn't think she would. Plus she's forgotten I had the geography exam today.

Mandy says if I think of anything I'm to phone, I tell her.

I don't have to rack my brains very hard to know why my sister's gone. I consider telling my nan, but what's the point; it's not going to get our Cara back.

Blow me down, but the day before my mam's due back our Cara rings up from a phone box and lucky it's me that answers my nan's phone in the hall. Cara's found a job with some film thing, she's only gone and met the Producer. Then—this bit whispered—she's sort of staying with him, he's rented them a bedsit in Notting Hill, just for now; don't say nothing, don't you dare say nothing, Cara says.

Have you gone daft? I ask.

Turns out he's way older than her, older even than our dad God rest his soul if that's where he went.

Don't say nothing, Cara repeats. This is for Your Ears Only. Then she says: Come down. Why don't you come down? What've you got to stay up there for? Go and get a biro. I'll tell you where.

I have to get away quick before my mam gets back. I change into my jeans, pack a quick duffle bag, take the 62 to Gosforth High Street, walk down to beside where the Town Moor meets the Great North Road except I'm going South. I stand on the kerb and stick my thumb out. Getting a lift is a piece of piss. Seven hours later a fat lorry driver from Paisley who stinks of BO and keeps on rubbing at his crotch drops me off at Finsbury Park and says Get the Tube from here-on-in lassie. He grabs a quick feel of my arse as I'm leaning over to open my door, sad bastard.

In the tube there's a big map on the wall and a skinny girl with dyed black straggly hair is standing beside it. She fishes a half-smoked fag out of her pocket and says to me Have you got a light. I hand her my book of matches. She lights the stub with a shaking hand then ambles off and keeps my matches. I watch her walk away. She's got no shoes on and her feet are filthy.

I stand staring at the tube map, trying to work out where to go. I follow the line from here to there with a finger: I'll have to go the blue line then change onto the pink. The blue line is the Piccadilly, so I follow the signs, head on through the tunnel and down and down the escalators with everyone rushing past. I had no idea escalators could go down this far.

They'd tried everything but nothing had worked.

It's no use, she said.

She was inspecting the light in the centre of the ceiling. The fitting had somehow got twisted, making the lamp hang at a strange angle, causing it to cast too bright a light on one side of the empty room, leaving the other side in shadow.

It's a trapezium, the man said. His voice was bright, echoey, there being nothing to absorb it.

He was looking at her looking up at the lamp.

Eh? she said.

Trapezium, he said. A quadrilateral with no sides parallel.

How d'you know that? she said.

He shrugged. I happen to remember, he said.

You remember the strangest things, she said, some really odd things. She gave a little snort.

He hesitated. Then he said, I remember, that's all. That's just how I am. Anyway, it's not odd. Trapezoid, that's what it is.

Oh, 'oid' now is it. And you always remember the wrong things anyway, she said after a moment.

She backed away from the middle of the room, her footsteps hollow on the floorboards. She came to rest in the shaded area, where she could look at the lamp from a different angle.

She pushed her hands further down in her coat pockets.

We'd better not leave it all bent, she said.

She went out of the room and came back carrying a

long wooden pole with a forked end like a snake's tongue. It was a prop that would normally be used for holding up laundry to keep it from trailing in dirt.

It's all I could find, she said, when she saw him looking askance at the prop.

She stood back the length of the pole and prodded at the light fitting. The lamp swung wildly, making random light and shade move up and down and across the walls. The room became a lattice of moving shadows.

That's no good, he said. We need to get hold of it at both ends, steady it.

Now it was he who went out of the room. He came back with a wicker chair, an old bathroom monstrosity of indeterminate colour, one whose seat had begun to unravel, its scuffed and faded legs dried up and looking ready to snap.

Nothing's gone right since we came to this flat, she said.

So you keep saying, he said.

He was positioning the wicker chair as near as possible underneath the light, which was a hit and miss thing, as it was still swinging.

It's hardly the flat's fault, he added.

So you keep saying, she said.

He stood on the seat. It creaked and shifted under his weight.

Hold it steady, he said.

After a moment, she stepped forward and laid one hand on the back of the chair. The other hand she kept in her coat pocket.

Placing his palms one on either side of the trapezoid shape, he pushed and squeezed, first from one end and then from the other, then top and bottom.

It's just making it worse, he said, letting his hands drop.

She let go of the chair and stepped back.

I told you, she said.

Don't start, he said.

I'm not starting, she said. It's you. You're about to go off on one.

I'm not 'about to go off on one', he said, mimicking, his face twisted. Listen to yourself, he said. If you could hear yourself. He shook his head, stepped down off the chair.

She walked over to the fireplace, which was made of marble. She traced her fingers along the thick gilded frame of the mirror that hung above it. Some chips of golden paint had flaked off, exposing a soft, white, chalky substance underneath. She began picking at it with her nails; more gold scrapings landed on the mantelpiece.

If you don't want this, she said, I think I'll keep it.

If you mean the mirror, it's not ours to want, he said. It's part of the fixtures. It was here when I came. It belongs here.

She stood up closer to the mirror and began pulling faces. She opened her mouth wide, examining her tongue and her back teeth. She clenched her jaw tight so the sinews stood out in her neck.

If the wind changes, you'll stay like that, he said. He picked up the chair.

It was his attempt at a joke. She started to laugh.

It wasn't that funny, he said.

No. I've just remembered something, she said. This mirror, it's made me remember something.

She laughed some more. Now she was looking at him in the mirror, looking into his eyes, looking right past her own reflection.

What? What did you just remember? he said. Come on. Share. Share the joke.

She laughed again.

That time, that time you walked, she said. She was laughing her way through the words. That time when you walked into that mirror! Smack! And you walked right into, into that massive great big mirror. In that theatre, she said, it was the King's Theatre. Oh my God, it was so funny. You walked right into yourself in the mirror!

Now she could hardly stop laughing. She turned round and faced him. The back of her head was in the mirror.

God, it was hilarious, she continued. I still can't believe you did that.

She continued to snigger.

He shrugged. He put the chair down, but his hands were still holding on to it.

Don't pretend you've forgot, she said, you can't have forgot. That has to be the funniest thing you ever did, she said.

He shrugged again, tightened his lips, fastened the middle button of his jacket.

She was having a sniggering fit now. She came right up to him, got hold of his lapels with both hands and waggled them backwards and forwards.

God, you were so funny, she said. Come on. You've got to see the funny side.

She let his lapels drop.

He moved away from her, out of the uneven glare of the lamp.

If you recall, he said, I actually hurt myself.

How can a person not see a familiar figure—I mean, themselves—looming right up to them, in a great big giant mirror? she said. Talk about not looking where you're going. She started laughing again.

Suddenly she stopped. She couldn't look at him, even though she wanted to. She wasn't laughing any more. She was standing there and twisting at the ends of her hair. He picked up the wicker chair and carried it out of the room.

It was Waiting for Godot, he says brightly when he comes back in. The play. At the King's. Waiting for Godot. We were waiting for Waiting for Godot. My turn to laugh now, he says.

A car's headlamps slant round the walls, then disappear.

Ian McKellen, he says, and Patrick Stewart.

I should know who it was, she says. It was me who got the tickets. It was me who booked the Travelodge. You don't have to tell me what bloody play it was.

A moment passes.

Sorry, he says. I mean, I really am sorry.

It had got very dark outside.

We'd better get going, he says.

When we leave, she says, there'll be no trace of anything that was ever us.

Only the lamp, he says, looking up.

Afterwards he asks me if I'm alright and I say, Yes, perfectly, but if it's all the same to him, I'd best be getting off. And he says, you know, he says, he's not like other blokes, he's not just one of those bastard types that just ups and leaves after.

Whatever, I say, picking bits of dead grass out of my hair. You could phone me, only you've took my mobile.

I'm starting to walk away but he yanks at my arm and pulls me back beside him, like he nearly pulls my arm out the socket, but I don't say nothing. He's laughing and he keeps on laughing while he fishes in the inside pocket of his leather jacket and produces a mobile. He waves it in front of my face.

Have this, he says. Swop. It's new. Brand new. Honest.

Honest.

He's holding the phone just out of my reach, laughing through his words. I don't reach out.

I'd rather have my own one back, I manage to say. I don't know how, but I manage to get those words out. My voice sounds amazingly strong. I'd rather have my own one, I repeat. You could …

No deal, he says, patting the pocket where he's stashed my phone. Serious now. He's still got hold of my arm. I'll get good money for yours, he says. But first I'm interested to see what you've got on it …

I try to snatch my arm away but he just grips on tighter. Half my life's on that phone.

What's the point in me having that one? I say. Dialogue. Come on. Try it. Keep going. Brave girl.

Have it, he says. He's bang bang banging his phone against my breastbone. Have it. And keep it on. I've got the number. I'll ring you.

I take it and put it in the back pocket of my jeans.

I'll walk you to the bus, he says now, walking more quickly, walking ahead of me, pulling me along behind him.

You don't have to.

I know I don't *have* to, he says, but I *am*.

He leans round and peers into my face. It's the first time I've looked at him, properly. He has the palest eyes you've ever seen, almost like they're not there, like they're trying to be absent. In the yellow glow from the street lamp, I see my own tiny-sized reflection in the black bit in the middle of his eye.

I need to get to the bus. I want there to be people.

The street's deserted, the only sound the soft squeeze of two pairs of trainers walking along the pavement, side by side, two into one. I realise he's synchronised, that he's put himself exactly in step. I hesitate a split second in order to break the bond. He puts in a quick extra step to even up and laughs again.

He doesn't speak. Nor do I.

I register that this is what it feels like to carry on.

We've passed the bus stop but he hasn't stopped, he's still dragging me along. Maybe he knows there's no night bus from here. He must know this route. I don't know where the next stop is, where the right one is, I don't know where I am.

You cold? he's asking, Have my coat. He's starting to take his leather jacket off.

I'm alright, I say, but I know I'm shaking and it's visible. I pull my sleeves down over my hands and tug at the welt of my jumper. My teeth click together as if I'm cold and even when I clamp them tight together they still don't stop. I am trying to nudge myself into a place where there's nothing, nobody, no bloody body, no body, body bloody no. I grope inside myself to disappear. He's taking off his jacket. He's letting go of my arm. I can get away. But no I'm literally frozen solid in ice.

Then, Budge! Budge over, will you. It's him, he's talking, he's elbowing me in the chest. Budge the fuck over, fuck you!

He's talking. Talking to me. I don't know what he's been saying what, how long he's been talking.

Fuck's sake, he's saying, get out the fucking way!

He barges me with his shoulder and, before I move over, for a moment, for a very brief moment, everything stills; before I move over, for one tiny moment, everything brightens, sharpens in 3D, then fades. I imagine a shiny black car accelerating towards us. A BMW. Series 5. One of the Brethren. Engine blasting loud through gaping pipes. A bank of front lamps, all full on. A black car, looming fast and loud. A big bass beat. You budge fucking over, I hear myself say. Then the thick grind of tyres on gravel. The driver changing down, straightening up, tyres spattering stones, accelerating off.

His words repeat themselves over and over inside my head. *Budge the fucking fuck over* and I'm stood there, alone, silent, staring into the road.

A phone goes. It's a moment 'til I register what it is, it's the one in my pocket, the one he made me have, vibrating.

Something comes crashing through and I'm on the edge of it, remembering.

Do it! Do what I'm telling you, right. What the fuck is wrong with you?

How easily his voice plays over. His voice is inside me. It's becoming my own.

I scrabble in my pocket for the phone. I'm on my knees. I was on my knees. He's holding my head. Pressing it down. Pressing it against him. Handfuls of my hair coming away in his hands.

She cannit even use a fucking phone!

No, I say, feebly. I'm trying to get on my feet again but my legs are not holding me. I sink back down.

Before, he'd called me a stupid ugly carcass of a bitch while I'd tried to dial help from my phone. I was pressing all the wrong things. I couldn't get the right buttons. He snatched it off me. I'd put up my hand to shield my face, winced, crouched. Then gave in, invited him. Cannit even use a fucking telephone, he'd mocked, afterwards. I said, I'm going to be sick.

Now I watch him getting smaller, dissolving at the edges. I stand under the street lamp and he's getting smaller and smaller and smaller until he's just a dot, then there's nothing. I throw his phone down into the road, hard, I hear it smash against the tarmac. I'm wetting myself and I can't do anything to stop it. I look across the road at the flats. There are still a few lights on. I count from the bottom. One two three four. The closest light is on the fourth floor. I won't make it.

Cara has just come in from work and still has her orange overall on. She looks at me but doesn't ask what I'm doing here. She lights a B&H and slumps down on the sofa, balances the ash-tray on her stomach. Look North is on TV, an appeal for witnesses, a hit and run in Leazes Avenue, in the early hours. A man critical. Father of two. Anyone with information should ring this number.

Poor bastard, says Cara, feeling down the side of the sofa for the remote. She flicks over onto ITV.

Fancy a Carlsberg? she says, heaving herself up.

Yeah. Go on. Pass us one of your fags while you're at it.

Cara gives me a long look. I can see she's about to re-mind me that I quit smoking months ago, but she keeps her mouth shut. Then, Help yourself, she says as she chucks the B&H over and goes to the fridge to fetch the lagers.

Lime? she calls through from the kitchen.

Aye, go on.

I light myself a fag while I'm waiting.

One evening I wrote a poem and I read it out to you and you said me dragging that old chair of your mother's into the study had scraped the floor and I realised my marriage was over.

Radio France Bleu Limousin was playing in the kitchen, some phone-in programme, crackly chat interspersed with music, mostly oldies. Your father's old clock was ticking its irregular tick. The dogs were lying by the fire and I'd forgotten to bring the candles in from the garden.

You were half-sitting half-lying on the sofa and your brown shoes, the ones you bought in Italy, were on the floor beside you, lined up, side-by-side. You'd picked up the Andrew Miller I'd recommended and the clock was ticking and your laptop was open on the table, the screen blank but the little blue light on the side was pulsing.

You were yawning and lying there stretched out on the sofa and you'd turned the standard lamp on, the one we bought from Emmaus, and some piano music started playing on the radio. One of the dogs got up, half-barking and the Andrew Miller you were reading cast a shadow on the rug, the one the previous people had left, and I could smell the garlic from the pasta I'd cooked earlier and I could smell the Camel you'd been smoking and you kept on yawning but they weren't ordinary yawns.

You were turning the pages of the Andrew Miller and you were sighing and someone was talking on the radio and the dogs were lying there with their heads between their paws, ears up, and you were half-sighing and half-yawning.

I was sitting in the green chair by the fire and that big log you had put on earlier was still smouldering. The heat was burning my legs even though I had my jeans on and you were half-lying down and turning your pages. A car went by and the noise of it echoed down the chimney and a dog up at the farm was barking and ours were listening but then they started barking and you told them to be quiet twice and you sounded very far away then angry. You carried on reading and our dogs carried on making little huffing sounds because the other dog was still barking.

Then there was a brass band on the radio and I thought you'd got up to turn it off but you put your shoes on and the dogs ran to the door both barking and half-jumping and you let them out and they were still barking then you went into the garden and closed the door behind you. I imagined you blowing the candles out and taking the key from your motorbike and putting it into your pocket and when the radio was playing something from Rigoletto you came back in and an owl was screeching as you opened the door.

You poured some wine, red for me and white for you, and one of our dogs jumped onto the old chair, the one that used to be your mother's and needed repairing, but you didn't tell him off even though his paws were dirty. You lifted the ashtray down from the mantelpiece and emptied it into the fire and lit another cigarette with the lighter you always had in your pocket.

Then you switched the radio off and double locked the door and put the key in the drawer where we keep the keys. And the clock was ticking but it hadn't struck yet and you sat down again but without opening your book and you sipped your wine and took short drags on your cigarette which was almost finished. I heard you blowing the smoke out because you'd turned the radio off and the dogs were being quiet except for one who was licking his paws which were damp from the grass outside. Another car went by and you stubbed your cigarette out in the ashtray then you picked up the Andrew Miller again and started reading.

Your shadow moved on the rug the previous people had left as you turned the pages of the book, the one I'd recommended. And the clock was ticking irregularly and the irregularity was obvious, no longer absorbed.

Then the pile of laundry on the back of the sofa suddenly toppled over and fell to the floor for no apparent reason other than an inherent longstanding imbalance I suppose. You were turning the pages of your book and the ashtray with the butt in was balanced on your stomach as the laundry toppled and fell quietly sliding to the floor like an avalanche.

Then you took your laptop and your wineglass and your cigarettes and you went upstairs. I followed you up, watching the backs of your trousers and listening to your shoes on the wood. You went into your study and you put down your laptop and pulled a chair in and then you started typing.

I went into the bathroom and put my pyjamas on. I opened the window wide and looked out at the clouds where they had cracked the moon right down the middle.

In bed I lay down beside where the moonlight was making a shiny patch on the bookcase. It was lighting up your Italian dictionary most of all and I could hear you still typing because you always bang quite hard when you type and it was beating against my breastbone like my heart was on the outside.

You coughed and you closed the lid of your laptop

then you looked for me in my study but it was the wrong room because I had gone into our bed. You came into the bedroom and you got in on your side and you lay there quietly not even making the sound of breathing. I was searching for some words but I couldn't find them and I wondered if you knew where they were, you with your talent for languages. But you gave no sign of any revelation.

I half wanted to touch you but touching the air seemed the only alternative. Lying on my back with my eyes wide open I saw only black because the moon had moved behind the poplars. I thought of the children, not that they are children any more, and of the mimosa we had planted and whether it would survive the winter.

The Big Man holds out his hand and Dolores presses the money into it, all of it, including the coins that were her own. She offers the remaining bundles of roses but he pushes them aside and stuffs the cash into his pocket.

Have a drink. He holds up a half-full bottle, no label. Smoke leaks from around the cigarette nipped in one corner of his mouth.

Sit down. He nods towards the far side of the table. Two—she'd seen those two before—move apart, their chairs scrape across the lino. They've made room, there's a gap, but no chair for her to sit on. She stands, her back to the wall.

I don't want to drink, thank you, please, her voice thin and far away. She wants to say she will go now, but the words don't come. No-one else is drinking.

One man pulls at his tie, another clears his throat, others shuffle in their chairs. No eyes are raised to look at her. This small room is stifling, heavy with cigarette smoke. Only one tiny skylight window, opaque, tight shut. The reek of sweat, beer spilled on another day.

The Big Man is handing her a grubby tumbler, more than half full.

Have a drink, he says again, insistence sharpens the edge of his voice.

She knows to accept the glass, put her lips to the rim. He will watch till she takes a proper sip, keep watching till she takes a bigger gulp. She leans back against the wall, feels the liquid burrowing hot all the way down to her stomach. She still has the flowers clutched next to her chest.

The Big Man now lights another cigarette and hands it

across to her. She puts the drink down to reach out for it. She puts the cigarette to her mouth, inhales. He watches, nods. She takes another gulp of the drink, another drag on the cigarette. The Big Man tops up her glass, sits down, pulls his chair in, shuffles the cards, deals.

One by one the men pick up, scrutinise, open and shut their eyes.

The Big Man rubs himself at the back of his neck, looks round the table, looking into one face then another.

Then the one with the eye patch—he's new, that one—half standing, half leaning forward, lets a handful of crumpled notes fall into the middle of the table; he drops back in his chair, wipes his mouth on the back of his hand.

The Big Man shakes his head. Pick it up. He nods towards the money on the table. Eye-patch looks around; no-one catches his one eye. But still, he lets the cash lie where it fell.

The Big Man reaches over and nudges the notes with the backs of his fingers. Pick it up, I thought I said.

Now the Big Man is looking straight at her, his gaze focused right between her eyes, the place to look when you don't wish to see a person.

No need for money, he's saying, not this time. The cigarette in the corner of his mouth moves up and down in time with his words. He's still looking at her, he's half-smiling, squinting his eyes against the smoke. No need for money. Is there, honey?

Dolores takes another gulp of the burning drink, then another, and another; she drains the glass. She raises the flowers to her face, closes her eyes, she breathes in deeply the scent of the roses. She tightens her teeth together, she looks back at the big man, she looks him in the eye. And she shakes her head.

Don't do that, please, the mother says.

The girl is scratching some sign or other into the gravel with a rolled-up umbrella.

How things have changed. My mother would never have said 'please' like that. Like she'd never have used coconut oil for frying.

That 'please' makes the difference between telling and asking. Are today's children fooled by the illusion they have a choice? Or perhaps the 'please' was meant for me, for my ears only. In which case I'm not duped either.

I continue on my way. Moments later the girl with the folded umbrella comes running back. She rushes past me. She runs across the tulipped lawn and disappears off into the trees.

Now look, here comes the dark-eyed mother. She comes striding towards me on the gravelly path. She's carrying her own rolled umbrella. She doesn't know which way the girl's gone, and she's not going to ask.

I head towards the café thinking I might find mother and daughter or one or the other and thinking about how girls shouldn't listen to their mothers for fear of repeating their mothers' mistakes and turning out to be not like themselves. If I see that girl again, I'll warn her.

The rain's drooped the daffodils onto the bark-chip path. The sun's out in patches. And this the place I once saw a goldcrest, only the second one I ever saw.

Oh, here they are again, mother and daughter, up ahead, coming round by the shrubbery, the mother carrying two umbrellas, the kid up front, kicking at the gravel with the toe of her shoe.

It's that slick bloke again. Table Five. The one with the eye-patch. I'm not serving him. No way.

Dolores has slammed so hard through the double half-doors, she's in the kitchen now and they're still swinging.

No way. You'll have to do him this time, Leroy.

Leroy looks up. He continues frying. Leroy's frying chicken. The corners of the pages of the recipe book he's consulting are all greased up. Leroy is following instructions to the letter. Oil hot. He lowers the floured and seasoned chicken bits in and they're spitting all over, cack-cacking like a BB gun. Leroy stands back, shoogles the pan at arm's length, tips it front to back and back to front again. Chicken bits are hissing, sounding angry. Leroy licks his thumb, flicks the page over, and back again. Dolores now, standing right next to him. Peering into Leroy's face.

Hello? Pause. Anybody in?

That stupid squeaky voice of hers. What the fuck? She's gone and stuck her finger into the French onion soup Leroy's got warming on the big back ring.

Dolores sucks her middle finger, sticks it in the soup again, looking directly at Leroy. She stirs her finger round a bit, grins, lick lick licks. Tongue curling out, wet, pink, purple.

Get yer filthy fingers out. Leroy shoulders Dolores out the way.

Dolores pulls a face, jabs the soup finger up in the air, in front of Leroy's nose.

Spin, Leroy, she sneers. She licks the finger. Long and slow.

Leroy puts himself between Dolores and the soup. Still holding the handle of the chicken pan. Still moving it a little bit this way, a little bit that.

Tastes shite anyway, Dolores says.

With his free hand, Leroy clatters a lid onto the soup pan. Not a bad shot.

Customers like it, he says.

Do they fuckry. What did he go and say that for?

Fuck the customers, Dolores snorts, 'specially that slick bastard on Table Five. I've told ya, Leroy. I'm not serving him. You can.

Leroy shrugs. That Dolores has way too much attitude, 'specially when it comes to Table Five. He picks up an open bottle of Merlot, sniffs it, glugs about a third of it into the chicken pan. Massive hissing, alcoholic steam clouds belching off. He checks the recipe again, turns the gas down, pulls the pan to the side a bit, takes a swig out the bottle before jamming the cork back in.

Dolores watching him, face blank.

Not paying attention today, are we Leroy?

Leroy laughs, shakes his head. That Dolores, she's something else. Leroy, now squashing fat cloves of garlic with the side of the big Sabatier until the skin pops off.

I heard ya. Leroy scraping mushed garlic off the board into the chicken pan. I heard, he repeats. Table Five. Dolores not serving. Eye Patch bloke who always asks if Dolores is on the Specials Board, Leroy chants. He laughs again. He likes that joke. That eye-patch bloke at Table Five's a bit of a wit.

Don't get cocky, Leroy. You're coming across a bit slick. Bit too much like that other one. Dolores steps away.

Dolores, now, standing in the middle of the kitchen, is stripping off her uniform. She's untied the little white apron with the frill all round, she's unzipping the little tight black skirt. She's kicked the high heels off, sends them skiting across the floor. Dolores, stepping right out of her clothes, letting them drop all around her. What's she on about? What's she on? Neat little black and white uniform landing in a crumpled heap on the greasy kitchen floor. OMG. She's serious. Off comes the tights.

Whoa…

Leroy stops what he's doing. He puts his up hands like she's about to shoot.

OK, OK, Dolores. Tell what's happening. I'm all ears. He wipes his hands on the tea cloth. What's with Table Five this time? C'mon, c'mon. I'm listening. You can tell Uncle Leroy.

Dolores continues undressing, taking off the white blouse, holding it out at arm's length between two poised fingers, looks Leroy in the eye, releases her fingers, lets the blouse drop onto the pile of clothes on the floor.

Leroy raises both hands in the air again, palms outward, backs off. Whoa, man! Sorry man. I never meant to offend …

Dolores, now down to grubby-looking brassiere and skimpy washed-out panties. God, she's skinny.

Fuck's sake, Dolores, get your kit back on.

Dolores bending over, gathering up the uniform, marches now to the corner of the kitchen, stuffs the whole lot in the bin, crams it all in on top of the remains of Table Seven's veggie lasagne. She claps the bin lid shut.

That's me, she says, matter-of-factly.

Dolores dusts off her hands, dramatically, one against the other, like she just finished a fight.

That's me, Leroy. Finished. Outa here. Finito. As I've

said before, Table Five can go fuck himself. I really mean it this time.

Almost naked, Dolores sashays across the kitchen, yanks black jeans and jumper out of the green metal locker, clanks the door shut so hard the whole row shakes.

Yes, fuck himself. And so can you, Leroy. Too sodding slick, the both of you.

She's serious. She's fucking serious.

I've had it up to here. Dolores gestures to her forehead.

Now she's pulling on the skinny jeans, sticking her arse out, sucking her belly in, edging the zip up.

Jeez. WTF. WTAF.

Leroy's making Dolores a coffee. Trying to make the peace. Dolores pulls on the black jumper, wriggles it down, yanks her bra back into place, pulls her cuffs right down. He hands her the cardboard cup and she's gripping onto it with both hands, like she's freezing. Are her hands shaking? Maybe it's just she's cold. Or is she coming down with something. What's the matter with her. Leroy half wants to know what's brought all this on and half doesn't give a shite. He's trying hard to give a shite. Dolores, she'll give him the low down, whether he wants to hear it or not. She sips at the steaming coffee.

That bloke on Table Five, right, he's reading this book, right, he's reading with his one good eye.

There she goes. That's her started.

And there's me, I'm standing there, next to his shoulder, where you're s'posed to stand, pad and pen, and I'm saying, you know, I'm saying, "You ready to order, Sir?"

He's not looking at me, for once, the rude bastard. Normally he can't keep his goggling eyeballs off and his nasty groping maulers—but no, I'm trying to serve him he's not even registering I'm stood there. So I'm saying again, louder, "Can I get your order, Sir?"

Dolores drains the cup and puts it down on the edge of the sink. She bends over and crams her feet into the baseball boots, first the left then the right. Tightens up the laces. Tucks the ends in. Pulls the jumper down over her arse.

In total, Leroy, she continues, I ask him three times, three times. "Is it your usual you're wanting, Sir?" This last time very emphatic. But Table Five just keeps on staring down at this bloody book he's reading, like his life depends. I've cleared my throat. I've moved to the side, I've moved smack into the field of vision of his one good eye. Nothing.

She's sounding genuinely put out.

Now I'm dying to see what book it is he's reading. I want to know what's so effing crucial he can't even soddingwell acknowledge my existence. I'm looking down at the book. I'm trying to see what it says. And as I'm looking, right, the words, the words in the book, right, they start dropping off the page. They're dropping off the page and landing on the table. Leaving little white gaps in the sentences. They're landing there, the words, on the cloth, the tablecloth, right in front of my eyes.

Leroy frowns.

Dolores nods her head.

I'm telling you, Leroy. I look away. I look back. I shut my eyes. I open them again. It's still happening. Leroy. Leroy?

Dolores tucks her hair behind her ears, picks up

the cardboard cup again. She's gripping it so tight, it's caving in.

I'm telling you Leroy, words are dropping off the page and, like, the man doesn't even notice. He's still reading. I look at his face. Concentration. I look at the eye, still tracking from line to line. And more and more words, dropping off the page, landing on the cloth, like little bony things, little tiny skeletons. They're piling up, the words are, one on top of the other, little piles of tiny insect skeletons, their legs stuck up in the air. Can insects even have skeletons? Dolores shrugs. Whatever. Then the words, they're crawling about, on their little skinny stick legs. they're marching off up the arms of the man's suit, little armies disappearing into his collar, trekking off round the back of his jacket, hordes of them, crawling over his lap and under his crotch and down his legs and up his nose and in behind his eye patch. And all the while their little mandibles are munching. Munch minch munch. Dolores bares her teeth, clashes them together. Listen. Can you hear them munching, Leroy?

Leroy breathes out, he looks at Dolores. He lays down the chopping knife, leaving half an onion half-chopped on the chopping board. He wipes his fingers on the cloth. He looks at Dolores again. He goes to the cooker, he lifts the lid off the pan, he stirs the chicken. She's lost it. She's totally fucking lost it this time.

Dolores looks at Leroy, shrugs, now she's picking up her satchel, straightening the strap across her chest. She's ready to go. Leroy should say something. But he doesn't know what. She's feeling about in her jeans' pocket. He should say sorry for last week, but she hasn't mentioned nothing so she's probably forgotten or doesn't want to be reminded. She's picking out coins for her bus fare. This could be his last chance. He should say something, but what?

Leroy lifts pieces of chicken one by one from the frying pan and dumps them into the casserole. Glances at the recipe book. His last chance. But no, she's not finished, not yet.

Reprieve.

And that's not even the worst of it, Leroy, you haven't even heard the worst bit yet.

Leroy picking stringy bits of thyme out of the pan, sucking the juice off, laying limp stalks on the side. He turns the gas up high. Keeps on glancing across at Dolores.

Table Five, Dolores continues, is being eaten alive, Leroy. As we speak, he–and I'm including here his nice navy blue sergey suit and stripey shirt with the plain collar, and paisley tie and matching socks, the plastic eye patch, the lot of it–I'm telling you, Leroy, the man at Table Five is being entirely consumed by tiny insect skeleton types that fell off the pages of the book he was reading. As we speak, Leroy, that is what is happening. Eaten alive.

Dolores nods towards the swing doors.

The slick bloke? Leroy doesn't know what else to say.

Dolores nods again, slowly.

Being eaten, you say?

Dolores nods again.

Leroy turns off the gas, strains liquid through a conical sieve into a clean bowl, pours it evenly over the chicken bits in the casserole. He puts on the lid. He turns off the soup. He takes off his apron, wipes his hands on it. Lays it to one side.

Eaten, you say? As in 'eaten'?

Dolores nods.

Go and see for yourself if you don't believe me, Leroy.

Dolores and Leroy, standing together in the swing doors, holding them open. There's no-one at Table Five. Table's empty. Leroy looks at Dolores, his eyebrows lift, he shrugs.

Told you, she says. Slick man. Gone. All eaten up.

Leroy shakes his head. He goes back into the kitchen. He puts his apron back on. He resumes chopping the onion. He's never liked that Dolores anyway. Not really. She's weird. He's no idea why he'd ever thought he fancied her.

On her way out, Dolores wanders over to Table Five. There's nothing left of the slick man, except an imprint of his backside in the soft faux-leather of the chair. The book's still there, lying on the table. Dolores picks it up. She opens it, flicks through. No title, no author, no nothing. Just blank pages. Not a word left in there. Dolores opens it wide, cracks open the spine, strokes the smooth paper with a finger. She leaves the book open on Table Five. The shadow of Dolores moves across the empty page as she pads across the worn lino towards the door.

Bye, Leroy, she shouts through. Have a nice life, won't you.

Back in the kitchen, Leroy jigging about to the tinny sound of Radio One, flicking through his recipe book, searching for a new dish to conquer. Words falling off the open page, but Leroy doesn't notice.

Jennifer's the one with the cackly laugh and hair the colour of polished conkers. You can tell it's synthetic. Her face has the eerie bland evenness of tone that the dead have, but she's the kind of girl who can wear red, and she does wear red, her dress is red, red velvet with matching knickers. Nicola—the baby—her hair is thick tight ash-blond curls, exactly the hair your mother wants. I covet it, she says, covet it. It sprouts up out of proper roots, no glue. I covet, you covet, he she it covets.

You want them dead and buried in shoe-boxes, But they're your babies, your mother says glowingly, they cost money.

You say, I'll have the money; kill them, kill them dead, give me the money.

Your mother knits pale rompers for the baby and spends hours smocking Viyella. For Jennifer, it's the red velvet dress and knickers, with a remnant. You are cut to the quick, the very idea of remnant.

In your pagan phase you give them woad with smudgy biro and nail varnish. Your mother removes it carefully with acetone while you sleep and sits them freshly laundered at the end of your bed.

You jam their little staring eyes shut with plasticine—they won't stop looking at you, following you around the room and making judgments—and you sit them facing the wall. You make the baby eat a pipe-cleaner. You stab at her wee-wee hole with a crochet hook.

Your mother picks the plasticine out of the eyelashes with a toothpick and shouts, How would you like it, if someone did that to You. You stand still and say nothing.

Your mother comes at you her lips so tight they've disappeared. She'll swing for you, she will, she will.

Night and day they smirked, the pair of them, day and night. Tight little painted mouths poised for mockery and insolence filled you full of dread and made you angry. Made you cruel. You locked them in the cupboard and left them for days on end and wouldn't listen to a single word they said.

After your mother dies you discover them crouched in the wardrobe where they must have been muttering for twenty seven years. You pick Nicola—the baby—up by her thick tight ash-blond curls and Jennifer by the burnished coppery tones and without so much as a glance at their shiny clean self-satisfied faces, you pop them into a Tesco's bag and throw it onto the skip along with the garden rubble and the remains of the kitchen.

In the night it rains and the red from Jennifer's velvet dress bleeds right across the baby's face but no-one's there to notice, no-one's there to care.

* what are you like *

Everyone says you're far too young, no good will come of it, no wonder your mother ended up in the state she did, poor thing, putting up with you.

When the baby's born the Midwife sends the Health Visitor and the Health Visitor sends the Doctor and the Doctor sends the Psychiatrist, Dr Porpora, to visit you at your flat. You realise with some alarm that his name is Italian for purple, though he's not Italian, he's from Glasgow; you don't know where that feeling of alarm comes from but it's there, it's real enough.

You will never trust the Porpora man on account of his excessively large thumbs. He has the biggest thumbs you have ever seen and you can't stop looking at them, the way he clenches his fists, thumbs pointing up, the way he moves his giant thumbs all the while he's looking you between the eyes and talk talk talking. You half want the baby to wake so you can leave the room and won't have to listen. You don't know what's worse, listening to Dr Purple or having the ravings of the baby pierce your skull.

The purple Doctor comes out with it, tells you: you've got an illness, Puerperal Psychosis—in its milder form, Post-Natal Depression, you've heard of it? Common enough, can be serious, extremely serious, (frowns, nods), requires treatment, yes, immediate. You understand? Do you understand what I am saying?

What you understand is this: The purple Doctor with the thumbs is saying there's something wrong with you. There Is Something. Wrong. With. You. Some-Thing-Wrong. With-You. There are risks involved.

The Doctor watches you wince. You, trying to stop the vomit welling up inside.

Just an illness. An illness like any other. Purple shrugs. No need to react like that. No need for panic.

You're having trouble taking it in. The Doctor's words bend round corners. Trickster words, shift, conceal. They're making you want to lie down.

There you are on your grandmother's pillow. Get to sleep when you're told. Before I tan your backside. I'm not telling you a second time.

Go now, Doctor, please. Go. The baby crying.

The man keeps on talking, talk talk talking: They can (will) Section you (Section: divide you in sections, cut you up in pieces). If you don't agree/won't agree, agree agree.

Agree with what? Is there a choice?

Hospital. Now. (Nods) Straight Away. (Nods) Treatment.

Treat-ment.

It all depends. He'll look into it. Trust him. In these cases, Treatment is needed, most definitely needed, definitely probably, sometimes, always, yes, needed. The Doctor will ring for the ambulance. Where's your telephone? Why don't you have a telephone?

You're trying to take it in, keep it out, assimilate it but it's invading you. You can't accommodate what the expert says without it becoming part of you and you can't have something wrong with you as part of you, it doesn't fit. Nothing fits.

Breathe in. Breathe out. Breathe. Just Breathe.

You need treatment. Think of the baby.

I am.

Well then.

I think of nothing else.

Well then.

Breastfeeding, those pills, they go into the baby's blood.

Put her on the bottle, a lot of mothers put their babies

on the bottle, it's perfectly safe, someone can look after her while you get the Treatment, have you got somebody to take her, yes we can help you, you must let us help you, for the baby's sake.

help help help

We wouldn't want to have to take the baby away

This Doctor, he says he's not a man for insisting, no, not like this under normal circumstances but this is not a normal circumstance is it, far from: it's a serious situation, the sooner you start taking it seriously the better, for all concerned, including the baby, especially the baby, like I say, we wouldn't want ... Now can we Please Agree on a Proper course of Treatment? Otherwise Dr Purple can't be expected to be Responsible for the consequences, no. This really is not the way he would ideally normally usually like to go about things, no it isn't, but this isn't an ideal world, is it, these illnesses, they get in the way.

In the way of Normal.

Think of the baby.

You hear her, you think of nothing else.

You can't stop staring at those giant thumbs; they're looming, growing, while the rest of the Doctor shrinks. The Doctor's voice booms echoes booms echoes across the pale miles of your kitchen, bounces off the distempered walls.

The Doctor Porpora beckons you close with a curling finger, confiding. He's brought paperwork (nods), he licks the thumbs with a wet pink tongue, uses the wetness to work through the piles of paperwork he's fishing sheaf by sheaf out of the smart leather briefcase. He's talking you through the paperwork, flick flick lick flick flick lick showing you the evidence, evidence, scientific evidence, proven, facts, facts and statistics, here it all is,

Puerperal Psychosis; puerperal means post-natal, after-the-birth, see, it's all in here. If you won't take it from him, here it is, in black and white, see for yourself, go on, take a look, look at the peer-reviewed medical journals the fat pink thumbs are thrusting at you.

Every time the doctor says Puerperal, you hear purple, purple insanity, purple psychosis, purple doctor room skirt purple attic. Where's my mother? We're taking your mother away. What's she taken? Blue ambulance light flashing purple under the streetlamp. Someone shaking you by the shoulder. What's she taken? Tell us what it is she's taken.

A baby crying, far away in another world, an infant abandoned, turns purple, murderous.

You sneak a look from behind your hair, you hiding from everything but a tiny fragment of this moment. Go on, do a normal thing, offer the good doctor a chair:

Do sit down, do please sit down, here is a chair.

The chair you offer is an aged wicker Lloyd Loom type that someone chucked away and you rescued from a life on the street. When Dr Purple sits on it, the chair gives way, the brittle legs splay. In the next room the baby ratchets up the scream. The chair cracks and collapses and smacks the heavy Doctor to the floor, broken beyond repair.

The Doctor picks himself up, heavy, dusts himself off, retrieves his glasses, says he's sorry, he should lose a bit of weight, eh, so sorry about the chair, can't understand it. He puts on the glasses, brushes himself off some more, gathers up his paperwork, pats and packs it back into some kind of shape. He'll replace it, yes, the chair, of course he will, you must send him the bill. Sorry, so sorry. He'll pay for the damage. The least he can do. Needs to lose weight, eh.

So many breathy apologies. The baby, squalling itself breathless.

Doctor Purple still talk talk talking, sorry, more than sorry, things way beyond sorry. He can't be any use to you now, he sees that, sorry for that as well.

You would go to the baby but you're torn ragged in pieces while the thumbs talk talk talk, wagging out the purple Doctor's story.

The thumbs want to do Obs and Gynae, they've had more than enough with Psychiatry, can you imagine, how hard it is, no offence but people don't realise, can you imagine what possessed the Dr to go into the purple profession dealing with crazy folk—sorry there, not a good word, no, no offence intended, but you know. It was his father, father's footsteps, that's what it was. These types of patient. Can you imagine. The Doctor shakes his head. These patients, sorry, but they make so many Demands. Enough's enough. Time to call it a day.

Your breasts swell hot and hard and heavy, your milk is finding its own way out, two spreading dark patches on the front of your teeshirt. You should go to the baby screaming.

Keep it, the Doctor says, hooking a thumb in the direction of the paperwork. You can keep it, the evidence, it's all yours. He mops his brow with a grubby handkerchief. I copied it for you. I won't need it now anyway not any more.

You nod, milk soaking your front now, two splatter patches spreading.

The Doctor won't be applying for any Sections. He smiles. He's sweating. His glasses have steamed up. You nod again. He says make an appointment you won't forget will you. You open the door. You don't know you're going to do it, but with both hands, your arms outstretched, and as hard as you can, you push the good Doctor out of the door and you clap the door shut behind him and put the chain on.

Lean your back against the door, breathe in, breathe out, and again, breathe. Now go calmly to the baby, little frenzied baby, frenzied deep purple baby.

Pick that little purple baby up, darling little one, so very small, such a tiny tiny infant, so very tiny, such little fragile bones, brittle little bones. She is yours. All your very own. Everything she's made of came from you, everything, everything, not a bit of her belongs anywhere but you. Hold her, hold her close, press her to your chest. Feel her suck the milk the life out of you. She sucks and gulps, gulps and sucks, pale sweet milk fills her mouth, drips down the little dimpled chin. Hold her close, hold her to your breast, closer closer press her to your chest, press her close to you, harder, press her harder, press her until she's quiet until she's still. There now, there now, all the breath's out of her and she's part of you again and this time it will never stop. You hold the little baby until she's gone cold.

Now look at you, look at the pair of you, in the long skinny mirror, you and the baby, lumped together, a single shape, squashed together, the two of you stuck together in one misshapen outline. Would you take a look at the pair of you.

what are you like.

When the near-dead arrive, men in transparent suits remove body parts and organs and fashion them into the likes of us. We could be sold for vast sums but the men who shave us from our keepers develop an affection for us and prefer to keep us for themselves.

We have no brain, or none to speak of. We have no need for brain; our bodies know all they need to know. Flesh memories dwell within us. Inaccessible, functional, curdled images and sunken stories of pasts–experienced and imagined–are codifed in our RNA where they constitute an essential substratum of certainty. Nourished by the emissions of our trusty mitochondria, our memories are the gumption that binds us together; we, the flesh musketeers. All for one and one for all, only a fool would deny we are each of us individual. She a vagina, he a bowel, me a spleen; we parade our uniqueness, we revel in it.

Some say we're vulval, but vulval we are not. We'll not be tooled into handbags, or stretched or pummelled or beaten and tanned into purses, embossed into soft covers, we'll not be scrimped into little drawstring bags for confining trinkets, never will we be conglomerated into fancy goods; none of this, not us. We're made of stronger stuff. We resist our fashionings when the mood dictates.

We're individual, singular, but we act in unison, which is where our strength lies. Together we can fight off any foe, any master, any blade or mace or spike or cleaver that comes slashing crashing pointing or slicing anywhere near us; we'll respond, we'll stand our ground, we'll say No and we'll be heard.

Some ask what use we are, if any. They ask if there's anything about us beyond what can be seen, anything important, significant, some hidden meaning, some purpose within or beyond our soft pink bodies. Fools! They say we're no more than severed superfluances, fleshy outcrops, that we're malleable, incidental, accidental, good for nothing but growing mould, gathering dust and wittering amongst ourselves. We speak. We speak our languages and only a few would guess the wisdoms that simmer deep within us. We're brimmed full of thoughts that twist at us from the inside, that make us curl and coil and lean and bend this way and that, like tentacles, picking up on currents, scouting everything out. We know. We know things.

There are always those who would slice us open, slice us with a will to conquer, a desire to dissect, an impulse to pull apart, dismember, twist and wrench, poke prod examine record. And when they think they've found out all there is to know they set to work on their shiny metal benches, with their measuring instruments and their fine glass vials and their sharp tools, their glues and their how-to manuals, and they reassemble us according to their own image.

Pah.

We prefer to rearrange ourselves, thank you very much.

We are the pink things, severed, we taste sweet.

Kit has a new girlfriend. Her name is Dolores. When Dolores asks Kit what he'd like to do for his birthday, Kit says a picnic would be just the ticket.

On the day, they pack up a picnic—or rather she does—and they travel down the College Valley to the foot of the Cheviot. They lay out the picnic—or rather she does—and Kit feasts on all his favourite foods, he drinks home-made cordial, and eats the final slice of home-baked birthday cake. Dolores makes him a pillow out of mosses and lichens and he lies down on the soft grass and falls into a deep contented sleep.

Kit dreams Dolores is clearing up the picnic things and weaving mountain flowers into a garland for her hair. As he watches, Dolores becomes almost a shadow, a mist that floats round about him. The pungent scent of the flowers soothes and enchants. Kit feels himself dissolving into the side of the mountain.

He wakes with a start. Dolores is gone. The picnic things are washed, dried and neatly stacked. He reaches out, sees his own arm, thin, brown, woody and twisted, indistinguishable from the roots of the heather.

In Sadie's room a stain was making its way up the wall. It began at the old covered-in hearth and it smeared itself into a darkening patch that had swelled and sent out pseudopodia which crept on up the wall.

She hadn't noticed it at first. Perhaps you don't notice, or Sadie had been distracted, attached no significance, which is how it is when you've moved into new rooms and you're grateful and there's luck to be had and baggage to be accommodated and nothing fits.

She remembers the day she unscrolled the old deerskin and stretched it out alongside the bed that for now was doubling up as a sofa. She'd piled up her books and notebooks in neat stacks ready, arranged some trinkets on the dresser. The rest would stay in the box. She would check them each week, devise new arrangements for familiar objects.

Then when she sat down to take it all in, the strangeness of the new, the comfort of the old freshly placed, it was then that she became aware of the stain. She was surprised to have not noticed it before. Now there it was and as clear as day and she couldn't not see it, it was pulling her eyes towards it, dominating her vision; there it was, marking its way up the wall and taking her with it.

She stared at it. The stain stared back.

She could swear it was growing, growing as she watched. But no, that wasn't possible. She'd need to chart it, chart it and measure it. She'd draw an outline and see how fast it was bursting its boundaries and in what direction/s.

She pulled herself up off the bed/sofa and went rummaging for a pencil. There was no pencil. She found an old lipstick in her box; that would have to do.

She confronted the stain, was tempted to stab at it but there was nothing to stab with. She wanted to slash it, pierce it, scrape it off, dig it out, cast it off, get rid. She stood back for a moment, pulling herself together; reasserting her purpose, she took the lipstick and calmly and carefully began to draw round the outline of the stain.

This is how Sadie came to discover the stain was growing, and in all directions. She kept vigil. Day and night it grew, she was certain. She had measurements to prove it. She wrote them into a notebook. She charted the stain's progress with the lipstick. She constantly tested the feel of it for damp with the backs of her fingers. There was a pulse, a definite pulse.

When her mother came she was carrying flowers. From the doorway she stared at the lipsticked wall. An orange speck of lily pollen flared on the lapel of her linen jacket.

Well I hope you're proud of yourself, the mother said.

* MIRROR *

When I looked in the mirror I saw my mother's face which is impossible as she is twenty years dead. And even before that, she wasn't there. Plus my mother would never have worn this black, this black that pales me. My mother was a woman for red, a woman who wanted to make a splash. All her life she drew blood though she had no teeth. My mother was determined, a woman of will. Now I see her willing herself back from the dead and up into my hanging mirror. I'll swing for you, she says.

He carved a house out of a giant bar of soap and lived there happily until the rains came and washed it all away. Never did a cleaner man lament the dissolution of a home. Never did a more hopeful man set sail for the faraway shores of Somewhere Else.

When he arrived, he found queues, dammit. He had to wait. For everything. His life became one long wait. Most days he spent leaning against the big flat window of the Starbucks on Buchanan Street.

A sorry sight, some say, shaking their heads. How come They get like that? Now you tell me how it is They let themselves get like that.

Some smile weakly–such a Waste, a Terrible Waste– as they exit through the swinging door and out onto the busy street, already sipping from their cardboard cups with plastic lids, seemingly in a hurry. He'd never understood that need to be in such a hurry. His head moves along with them, his eyes track their feet; since he arrived he's seen all manner of feet and shoes hit hit hitting the pavement in rhythm, with purpose, intent, deliberation. The feet pass him by, and he knows the precise spot where their steps will slow, the hurry seeping out of them, like they're recovering from being winded, the way their shoulders rise and drop, big new breaths audible then dissolving. Suddenly they're taller, back in their own lives, out of his.

Mostly though he's invisible, transparent as the sneering Starbucks' glass that doesn't even throw him back his reflection. People on the other side are different. Look at them, the people on the inside, drinking their chai skinny lattes, if you can imagine wtf is that. Look at them chatting smiling tap-tap-tapping on their laptops, frowning into mobiles, eating cupcakes, hugging damn them, hugging. But for the glass, he'd be rubbing shoulders with that one there with the tousled hair.

Oh, it was cold that winter. Yes yes, you'd known it colder, but this was different. This was cold that made your bones spike as though already stripped of flesh. The sleeping bag was useless, worse than. You'd even piss yourself on purpose for the warmth of it, for the stinking comforting wet warmth of it. Did you survive that winter? Something did, you're not sure what. When someone shook you by the shoulder and asked your name, you genuinely forgot that questions of that sort required answers. Anyway you didn't know the answer. You thought they were offering you a dog and you shook your head then closed your eyes.

Early morning thick winter morning on Buchanan Street, it's barely light, puddles iced crack with the wheels of wagons that come to unload, engines left running, the stench of diesel. And off the back of a low-loader the world arrives in a large cardboard box: 'Main Bulk,' 'Fragile,' and 'This Way Up,' in great red letters all over the sides.

Ah, but some fucker's ignored the instructions, some clever fucker's put the world upside down.

A mother hid among law books in a library. The dusty tomes shed their pollen like lilies. Squeezing her narrow body between the cold metal uprights, she set herself up alongside *Gadalmer & Glendinning on Tort*. She sat up, her spine straight, she didn't eat for days. When she spoke, her voice was the papery sound of pages turning; faint wafts of air her breathing.

When they came to turn off the lights she stayed hidden on the shelf. There, up there, can you see the marks she made in the dust?

When morning came there were only books. The stooped librarian passed along the shelves and counted, as usual, one by one, the volumes in his care. He came to the mother and he did not pass her by but touched her yellowing leather spine with a finger of welcome. He made a note of the new arrival for entering into the system.

The children all said, Ah but where is our mother?

Then when they received the letter on headed embossed archive paper, they said again, Where but where but where is our mother?

And they went to the library and they climbed up all the stairs of the dusty building and the librarian said, You have a request you say, if you could just fill out this form, and fetching time is fifteen minutes.

The words my mother said, I kept them, I made a list, I added to it daily. At first just singletons, a few small phrases. Then things, I listed things, the things she hoarded: mostly toys, her brother's, broken. I crammed everything into the box that used to be for fuse wire, tacks, screws, nails. I fixed a metal clasp on and jammed the lid shut. Just in time. There was a lot of noise: my mother's voice, and all the other stuff clamouring, hammering, yammering, bashing at the sides. And that old box rocking about like a jumping bean.

For safe keeping, I left the box on a shelf with a big stone on top.

Every now and then I'd have a little look, a little listen. I might detect a low level electrical hum—that had to be the new Kelvinator, 1962. Or water moving—the river at the foot of Ben Nevis, the way it rushes down the glen after the melt, swirling copper brown round the feet of the alders. Or there'd be a sticky sweet almost sickly smell—Candy Floss from the Hoppings; spun sugar, tastes nice but rots your teeth.

The box had been quiet for several weeks. I was looking at it sitting there on the shelf with its stone on top and before I knew what I was doing, I had lifted the stone off, laid it to one side and I was standing there, expecting something to happen. Nothing did. There was no movement, no noise. The box was docile. So I undid the clasp. I opened the lid a fraction. I put my ear to the opening. It was quiet and still. So I allowed myself just the tiniest, the quickest wee peek.

No sooner had my squinting eye drawn level with the slit of an opening than I was overwhelmed with a sensation, a peculiar sensation I've not known, before or since, which makes it difficult to describe. It was like longing but it was not longing. It caused my insides to flinch and to stay flinched. It was like a yearning that had no object or reason or purpose. It was wet and raw and stripped of civilisation.

The frantic buzzing of a bluebottle caught in the cobwebbed skylight of my attic pulled me back from the strange place to which the box had taken me. My only thought was to clamp the lid back on. I don't know how long that took, the trapped creatures fought me all the way, hissing and snapping, cajoling and pleading, snarling abuse. Finally I got the clasp done up. I sunk back exhausted, while in front of me on the floor the box jiggled and jumped and cursed out all manner of vile accusations. The next hours I spent fitting a second, stronger, clasp. And then I put on a third, and a metal band, padlocked, which took me well into the small hours.

A solid dreamless sleep and I woke to the knowledge of Things crawling over me. I could feel them on the bed, under the covers, jostling around my head on the pillow. I leapt up, afraid that at any moment I'd be suffocated.

Immediately I saw it—the lid of the box was flung open, its clasps wrenched apart, its hinges twisted. The box was tipped over on its side, empty. Its contents swarmed about the room, squelching and cackling. The whole place was stinking of herring guts and creosote and ironing, mothballs, liver and onions, perm lotion and Elizabeth Arden Blue Grass. In my mouth I could taste those thick brown drops my mother always took to help her manage. The old toys of her brother's she'd clung onto all those years–tinny wind-up things–were clicking and marching and tumbling on their sides, whirring staccato and rusty through their paces. Dolls with cracked ceramic faces and stained cloth bodies lay slumped in piles, their blank eyes staring, their legs and arms at all angles. But worst of all were my mother's words. They were crawling round over everything, millions of wiry little specimens speeding up and down the walls, scuttling in and out of everywhere, hissing and cursing. Vehemence spattered the walls, piles of disappointment congealed in corners, envy oozed into the woodwork, clagging up the door frame, dripping through the floor.

Clara says: why not write a letter to your mother. Put in all the words you could never say to her.

Ok, I say. But then I get stuck on the first line. What am I supposed to put after the 'Dear'? I can't force any of the usual words out, I just cannot.

Ah, says Clara, let's take it from there.

Clara is a strange fish. She wears odd shoes, different colours, one red, one green. She sits on the floor, under the window where the light is such I can't make out her face. In its place is a darkness, a silhouette, with wild curly hair. Clara's legs, in crumpled linen trousers, are hugged up against her chest so the shoes point across the room towards me, openly declaring their distance and their difference. I am conscious of my own feet facing hers across the no man's land of the stripped pine floor.

I buy some strappy fuck-me shoes that I can hardly walk in and I team them up with the short black PVC coat, genuine retro—I'm old enough to own the real Mc-Coy. I pull the belt tight French style and tie a knot. I put the dark glasses on. It's difficult getting up Clara's stairs with the shoes and the glasses on, but I manage.

What d'you think you're playing at? Who the hell do you think you are?

Clara stares at my shoes, plus I've left the coat on and I'm sitting on the chair instead of lying on the couch.

You're spineless. No backbone. Touched, that's what you are. You need your head examined.

We sit for a little while in silence. The fact that I am paying dear for this makes me the first person to speak.

I couldn't write to my mother, I say, but I put all her words in a box.

There she goes again, listen to her, making her mag go, mouth like Tynemouth. I'll give her something to whine about.

In a box, says Clara.

Yes a box, I say. But they've burst the lid off and they've all got out. They've taken over my life, I mean my attic. It's a question of how to get them all back in. Into the box. I need help.

Tell-tale-tit, your tongue shall be slit, and all the little dickie birds ... Knock your teeth down your throat, that's what I'll do, that'll shut you up.

On the wall to the right of me is a picture of the sea looking wild and unpredictable, you can almost hear it hollering.

Behind the couch is a smaller painting of a harbour, little coloured boats tilting at all unlikely angles, like they're about to tip out of the canvas and clatter all over the floor.

Do you want to go on the couch, Clara asks when she sees me looking over in that direction.

I'll murder you. I'll swing for you. Nasty little liar. Get out of my sight.

The blue and white boat in the foreground is called *Our Girls*. It's been pulled up out of the sea and is stranded alone and precarious on the pebbly shore.

No, I've told you, I say, I don't want to go on the couch.

I've never wanted to lie on that couch. I take my coat off, lay it over my knees, hold onto it.

This is my mother's cardigan, I say. She knitted it.

Don't you dare touch anything of mine. Keep your filthy hands off.

She made it for you, says Clara.

No, she made it for herself.

But you're wearing it, says Clara. I thought you gave her clothes to Oxfam.

I did, but I kept some.

It's hard to say goodbye to her, says Clara.

I curse the day you were born. I'll be glad to see the back of you.

She's been dead three years, I say.

All the same, says Clara, pushing her legs out straight and rubbing her knees.

There's an enormous bunch of white lilies on a tall table in the corner by the window near where Clara sits. Their scent is strong; I smell it over here. They are wide open, the flowers, screaming. There are always fresh flowers in Clara's room. And little piles of smooth stones. Like eggs. On the hearth.

Lilies. For purity, I say.

What do you want to wear your mother's clothes for, asks Clara.

How d'you think I might get all those words back in the box, I ask Clara.

You could start by putting the clothes in, Clara says.

She wants to strip me naked, so I'll oblige.

Give me a box, I say, I'll put them in, here and now.

I start pulling the clothes off and soon I'm starkers, except for the shoes still on. Clara is impassive and I'm stood there, naked. I sit back down. The fifty minutes will soon be up, and what will she say then. Will she let me flounce down the stairs in only the shoes? Stumble down her street with nothing on?

Clara chances a glance at the little clock she keeps near her.

How does it feel, to be so exposed, she asks.

You promised me a box, I say, but you've let me down, you've let me down, you always let me down.

I'm on your side, she says.

Is this a game of ping pong, I ask.

Ping pong, Clara says, as though it's a question.

Ping pong, I say, in the manner of an angry statement.

Clara and I are looking at each other's shoes.

You're wearing odd shoes, I say.

Yours are a little odd too, says Clara. She almost smiles.

Odd, I say, with the question inflection.

Yes, says Clara, yes. She glances at the clock again.

The box, I say, I need the box.

I'm all out in goosebumps. I should warn her, I could be sick.

Your mother's dead, Clara says. You've buried her.

Yes, I put her in a box and I buried her.

Clara gets up and hands me a tartan blanket.

You can let her go, she says.

I put my things back on, everything except the cardigan. As I turn to go, I bundle the cardigan under the seat, take a last look at the painting of the harbour. All the little coloured boats, all so safely moored, Our *Girls* pulled up there, on the pebbles, by the road.

Sadie had stepped out of her comfort zone but it was cold out there so she went back in. But whilst momentarily out there on her own dear safe threshold she'd glanced across the blank bleak tundra and across the waste she'd glimpsed a tiny pinpoint thing moving across the horizon so close to the ground. It was creeping, creeping along ever so slowly like a belly-down animal that wished it could conceal itself completely.

The image stayed in her eye after she'd gone back inside, after she'd closed the door and drawn the bolts, after she'd turned the great old key in the ancestral deadlock, after she'd gone from room to room turning on all the lights, all the lights, lights on shining shadeless in every room.

The image stayed and it seemed imprinted, it had taken its place on the back of her eye like it had rights and entitlements, like it belonged. Day after day she was reminded of its constant presence, always there when she was trying to look normal, when she was trying to look at her normal usual things, there it was, superimposed.

Sadie mentioned it to no-one but its persistence puzzled her and made her think of grains of sand or grit; it made her think of the grey sturdy-shelled oysters on the white plate on the little table by the window with the red-and-white checked table-cloth at the Restaurant Polidor in the Rue M. le Prince, her favourite restaurant in Paris; it made her remember that time she lost her glasses at Schiphol airport and how she'd walked off with someone else's baggage in the hotel in the Dordogne, and the other time going from Rome to Milano how she'd missed the plane and Cara entirely, she didn't know how.

No, having all the lights on is doing no good at all. Sadie goes now from room to room one by one switching all the lights off. She closes the curtains to keep out the street-light. She has blackout blinds installed. She ties a black silk scarf round her eyes like a blindfold and stumbles about in the dark crashing into furniture and knocking things over and stuff's getting dropped and spilled and chaos could be taking hold. It becomes safer to stay in bed.

But at the end of her bed in the long dark of her room still the horizon looms with its small pinpoint of light, creeping along, ever so slowly.

In summary, the information we have is this: In the cupboard at the top of the stairs they find a skeleton hanging where it had once been hanged; owing to the complete absence of flesh, the noose no longer taut, the skull tilted at an angle of 47 degrees. Some of the bones appear to have been broken and their jagged ends fixed together with wire–now considerably rusted–so the usual anatomy of the human is altered and now incorporates some odd bone angles, the whole somewhat resembling a marionette. There has been much material disintegration. Such time has passed as has led to some degeneration of the structure and some powdering of the bone—observe how it leaves traces on your fingers, not unlike talcum.

The way they jostled and pushed each other on the stairs:

Me first
No me
I'm the oldest
It's not fair, I'm always last

But things only remain true for so long and many patterns fade with time, so Sadie it is who this time stands back at the foot of the stairs and invites Cara to lead the way. Sadie follows Cara's ample ironed linen rump up the stairs. Cara stops at the top before the big wooden wardrobe. Sadie stops beside her. Sadie and Cara, side by side, are facing the door.

Cara's long pale carefully-manicured fingers reach out and manoeuvre the awkward handle–it was always awkward–with the confidence and expertise of one calm through practice. The lock springs open with click—a bright, youthful click that belies its age. They step back as the door swings open on its hinges releasing familiar smells of unpainted wood and dust and the sound of mother yelling up from the kitchen *Don't you bloodywell dare.*

The door wide open and there it is, dangling, its wrists and ankles bound with garden twine—browned, fraying, fibrous, unravelling, unspinning, spiraling undone, but still connected. Cara's carefully manicured left hand moves to her face, goes to cover her open lipsticked mouth. Her right hand reaches to the side of her, catches hold of Sadie's arm just above the wrist.

Sadie pushed Cara down the stairs and made her fall. Made her fall down down and her ankle broke. She was lucky it wasn't her neck.

Don't tell, don't you dare tell. I'll kill you for ever if you ever dare tell. You're lucky it wasn't your ruddy neck.

I fell off the slide in the park Mam, cross my heart, cross my rotten heart, Mam, I fell off the slide.

She couldn't walk, Mam. I piggybacked her all the way home.

This little piggy went to market

This little piggy stayed at home

This little piggy had jam and bread …

Honest Mam, I carried her, I carried her, all the way home.

Honest Mam. Listen Mam.

Laboratory analysis reveals: In the bone powder, traces of calcium, magnesium, and lead. [Footnote: the levels of magnesium are extraordinarily high and the presence of lead anomalous].

[Something illegible] … indicated here by pitting, the bones are porous as is to be expected in bones of this age [Footnote: porosity may also reflect prolonged exposure to the elements, or? possible radiation?]

Liars liars the pair of you nasty little liars
Rotten to the core
I'll murder you the pair of you
I'll swing for you I will

Cara looks at Sadie. Sadie looks at Cara.
It's time.
After a moment, Sadie nods.
Yes. It's time.

Cara removes her manicured hand from her made-up face, straightens herself up, tugs down her pale linen jacket and leans forward into the cupboard. With one hand she reaches out to touch the wires which stirs the puppet bones, ever so slowly, they begin to move. And they're wind chimes, they're music, they're the mobile in the nursery turning gently in the breeze from the open window.

And here comes the marionette again, here it comes stiff-limbed from behind the curtain when all the lights are out, here it comes to dance its stilted steps, here it comes to sing

Go to sleep, go to sleep, go to sleep my little darlings

Continuation of the laboratory analysis: It would appear that, at some point, the bones have been bleached. Possibly washed down with peroxide. Which accounts for their extraordinary whiteness. Peroxide penetrates and continues to bleach for many years after the initial application provided the bone is left undisturbed. The only slight yellowing ... [illegible]

You sure?
Sadie nods.

You sure you're sure?
Sadie nods again. *Let me*

Sadie tugs at the pressed sleeve of Cara's pressed linen jacket but Cara doesn't respond.

I said let me

Sadie has to pull hard on Cara's arm to jerk Cara out of the way. Then she has to nudge her hard with her shoulder. Then she has to barge her to be able to put her body, her big fleshy body, between Cara and the skeleton in the cupboard. Sadie now stands between them. She would stand there forever between them.

Mam, our Sadie's barging in
Tell tale tit
Your tongue shall be slit
And all the little dicky birds
Will have a little bit

Sadie it is now who stands in front who now reaches into the cupboard who now with one swift flick of her hand on the knot undoes the noose, and causes the bones to clatter to fall to the floor and scatter and the dust to rise. And, after, the silence. The dust settles in the silence and the sisters leave.

To quote from the report: "The bones appear to have been well-cared for. The skeleton appears to have been tended, tended includes as regarding, at some point, the careful paring away of the mother's flesh."

Look. Here he comes. Here comes Billy, bumping that old hand-cart over the cobbles of Back Stepney Bank.

The winter evening's drawing in and Nellie Grainger waits, standing by her window at number 5. She pulls the net curtains a little to one side and looks out into the dark. She's heard the cart. Yes, it's him. Here he comes. So, he has been out today, Billy Walker, out on the rounds, today of all days. Nellie lets the nets drop back into place. She presses her lips tight together, she shakes her head, she glances at the clock, it's nearly 5. He's back a bit sharp tonight, and no wonder. He's too old by half for keep on doing this lumber malarkey is Billy Walker, but he will keep on, he's not stopping for nobody. Nellie shakes her head again. There's never been any reasoning with that Billy Walker. A'ways been a law untiv 'isel'.

The wind's getting up, Nellie hears it rushing down the chimney, she'll need to shut the damper down or the fire'll burn itself out. But Nellie doesn't move immediately. She stays behind her nets till Billy's cart comes rattling past her door, then she picks up the scuttle and tips the last of the coals onto the fire. She'll go out in a minute and get a few more coals to keep the fire in for the night.

Piled up on Billy's hand-cart are bundles of rags, tangles of scrap iron, old electricals. Billy's round, up and down the steep back-to-back red brick terraces of Raby Street, Byker Bank, all of it, Billy's patch.

Any old lumber? Every twenty paces. The call's become part of him, it's all of him, it's none of him.

Any old lumber? Stockingless women in bulging slippers wait on doorsteps to hand over armfuls, *Glad to be shot of it,* they say as Billy takes the stuff, hoys it onto the cart, touches his cap and ambles on.

Any old lumber? The rattle of cart wheels, doors bang shut behind him, Mondays to Thursdays, always the same. Fridays, it's the slaughterhouse to collect the bones.

When dusk draws in, Billy lugs the hand-cart—heavy on good days—back over Byker Bridge, takes a sharp left, then bump bump bumps his way down Stepney Bank. Billy's hands in the worn grey mittens—knitted many moons since by the good Nellie Grainger—grip tight now on the smooth wooden handles. He's breathing hard, breath after breath puffing out of him in the winter evening air.

Stepney Bank is steep and Billy cannit have that auld cart running away with itsel'. Imagine, if he let go of it, imagine it gannin clankin' over them cobbles, all the way doon, tipping all the stuff off, bumping and dunching, imagine it, that auld hand-cart finishing up, wheels a-spinning, upside doon in the stinkin' river.

Billy with cold hands holds on tight.

Look at it down there, the filthy Ouseburn, opaque and grey, slakey as a dead man's eye. Look at it lurking in the valley bottom, just waiting for Billy to leave go of the cart.

But Billy's hanging on, holding back the weight of it, he's hanging on like he always does, steering the auld cart as best as he can.

Drawing level now with the row of higgledy-piggledy cottages that cling onto the bankside Back Stepney Bank and there's old Nellie Grainger as per usual lurking behind her nets, the nosey besom, she thinks he cannit see 'er, but he can. Billy won't tip his cap, not the day he won't. With numb fingers, he hangs onto the cart, stops a moment to catch his breath, hears in the distance the long blast of the Tynemouth foghorn. Aye, the fog'll be up soon enough.

Yes here it comes, here comes the fog, and it's a big one. A thick sea fret slides in on the tide, getting thicker as it makes its way up the Tyne. See it pushing its way along by the shipyards, past the quays and the staithes, thick and grey now as it passes the docks, the wharfs and the warehouses, before it seeps across the Middens and hunches its way up the Ouseburn towards where Billy is standing. It's reached Lime Street and now here it is coming up Stepney Bank. The fog arrives and gathers under the great arches of the viaduct, mixed now with coal smoke and all the industrial debris that make the whole lot of it sink around Billy under its own grey weight. Billy has to cough to clear his chest before he can pull and shove and heave the cart the last few yards and yank it round to line it up with the arched wooden doors of the cart-shed.

Howway Billy lad, get a move on, ye need to get in oot o' the cauld, afore ye catch ya death, man.

But Billy's freezing fingers aren't working, he's having trouble steadying the cart while he fumbles with the padlock. The key skitters and skites over the hole before he manages to jam it in, then it needs some coaxing before it'll turn. Billy should have oiled it long since, but he's had other things to think on. The lock comes away suddenly and Billy yanks the rusty chain a-clattering through the cart-shed handles where the paint's all worn away, dark green paint, from way back when, and it reminds him... and before he can stop it, the tune starts up in Billy's head:

Golden slumbers kiss your eyes
smiles awake you when you rise
sleep little darling do not cry and I will sing a lullaby …

and it's the voice of sweet Mariah Tulip, singing by the cradle, to the rhythmic creak crack creak as the cradle swings.

Here, where Billy now stands in front of the cart-shed, here the very spot where the old man Tulip used to work his anvil. *Thems were the days, eh, when this old cart-shed served its time as the blacksmith's place and Billy had been the favoured one. There was horses then, a-plenty, you didn't have to pull the ruddy cart yersel'.* And young Billy Walker, yet wet behind the ears, how he'd loved that fire at the forge, the heat and the glow of it, the terrible roaring power of it, and the noise of the giant bellows working, drowning out the foghorn, drowning out everything, and the smell as the molten iron shoes hissed hot on the horses' hooves. Those great horses, with their massive tufted feet and Roman noses, it always amazed Billy how they just stood there, eyes half shut, and let it all happen. *Aye, there was horses then in them days, horses. And hopes an' all.*

See this old horseshoe, the one on that door there, the great big one, the old man Tulip gave that to Billy when he was just a wee bit bairn.

Mind ye keep it the right way up lad, the old man had said, *ye divvent want all ya luck fallin oot.* And he'd dusted it off with his big leathery hands and handed it over. Billy had accepted it proudly, a muckle geet big thing it was, so heavy he'd hugged it to his chest to keep it from dropping it and tipping all his luck out.

The memory makes Billy close his eyes; how memories make things real again, how close they bring things, like there's been no time passed in-between, like what mattered then still matters now, like everything else is nothing.

All those dreams and promises. Billy could've done anything, that's what the old man Tulip said, anything. And he'd promised him; all this, he said, the shed, the forge, the furnace, the lot if it, all to be Billy's when the old man passed on. And his thick weathered arm had swung around, swooped over everything, *all yours lad the lot of it, Yours lad, when you're man enough,* the old man Tulip had said. Billy was then barely ten-year-old and people were saying *that's what you was born for laddie-o,* born for, to work those bellows, to forge that iron. And Billy had looked at the old man and seen his own face shining happy in the roar of the fire.

Both doors are open now and Billy tugs the laden cart the last few feet into the shed. He's got the rags to sort, then he'll have a bite to eat, there's a bit mutton stew left over, mevvies a chicken wing. Billy pulls the doors to, lights the paraffin lamp, gets the stove stoked up, puts the kettle on, sits down and lights a Woodbine. He'll keep his coat on till the chill's off. That wind's got up again, juddering at the doors, rattling the old tin roof. Billy sits on, smoking, watching the flames take life. He's tired, so tired. There's comfort in the familiar smells of the fire, of Woodbines, the rags, paraffin, even the stinking barrels of bones.

Sleep little darling, do not cry… And I will sing a lullaby

Billy wakes with a start to the sound of singing and, as if far away, a bairn wailing. He hadn't meant to nod off. The kettle is rattling, hissing steam and spitting boiling water. Billy heaves himself out of the chair. Between his yellowed fingers, he's still holding the burnt down

Woodbine with its hanging column of ash. He lets it drop and grinds it into the dirt on the cart-shed floor. The damper's been open far too long and the fire's roaring like the devil, like the old man Tulip's furnace used to roar. Billy gets a jemmy and bashes at the hot metal damper to close it down; that should fettle it.

But that bloody bairn, it keeps on wailing, and Billy keeps on hearing it, and it seems to be getting louder, and he's hearing it even above the roar of the fire and the rattle of the roof and the cart-shed doors in the wind. He can hardly stand it, but there's nowt he can do about it, and he knows it, not now, not ever. He'd best just get on with things, get them rags and bones sorted. Was a time when he did them every night, religious, but he's got behind, and there's stuff piled up all over, waiting to be shifted.

But the heat in here, and that blasted bloody racket. That blinkin' bairn and its incessant wail, it's getting closer, you'd think it was being murdered, what a carry-on. He really can't be doing with it, not any more, not today of all days. Billy shoves at the pile of rags with his leg, pushes it to one side, heaves opens the door and steps out into the night.

Outside: thick dark smoke from his fire drifts on down, mingles with the fog, surrounds him damp and heavy. A goods train lumbers noisily over the viaduct, dropping smuts and hissing steam. Billy lights another Woodbine, sucks the warmth of it deep deep down, deep down, as far as it will go.

A night it was, a cold night, a foggy night, a night just like this one, exactly thirty year ago it was when Billy lost wor Mariah. Thirty year Billy's been by hissel', lugging the old hand-cart, doing the bones and the lumber and not getting no help from any bugger. Billy exhales smoke, takes another deep drag. Outside, the same sweet-ish sour smell of malt and hops from the brewery, the same flickering halos of yellow light along the river, the same bairn wailing. Twenty-nine year old, Billy Walker was, Mariah Tulip barely sixteen. The wind is blowing a fine rain now, it pricks at Billy's face, and stings at his eyes. He tramples his cigarette end into the dirt, picks up the broom and sweep sweep sweeps mechanically at the wet cobbles in front of the shed.

At number 5 Back Stepney Bank, across the way, Nellie Grainger is busying herself. She knows full well what day it is and she means to keep herself busy and her thoughts at bay and if Billy Walker had any sense he'd be doing the same. Nellie's set the table for the lodger's breakfast, she's put the clean cloth on, she's laid out the cup, the saucer and plate, the knife, fork and spoon, all ready for the morning. She'll fetch them coals in and bank up the fire before she turns in and she prays that nothing, please God nothing, untoward.

Nellie undoes her pinnie, hangs it on the back of the scullery door, she pats the back of her thin white hair, picks up the empty coal scuttle and goes out into the yard. There's a light on over yon at Billy Walker's. And Nellie can hear him hacking and barking. His chest's not good and he's got it bad tonight, the poor beggar. Nellie fills her coal-scuttle and is about to go back in. Just as she's pulling the coal-house door to she hears it, the wailing, she hears the bairn wailing, the same as she's heard it those times afore, there it goes again. Nellie listens. It's the bairn sure enough. Nellie Grainger crosses herself. Then she dumps the coal-scuttle in the yard and rushes to get the stool steps so she can get a better look over the wall. She climbs up and she sees it, something she's not seen before: In Billy Walker's cart shed, in front of the roaring fire, there sits Billy Walker, and on his lap a baby, a baby swaddled in filthy rags and it's suck suck sucking sugar-water from a twisted scrap of butter muslin and looking up straight into Billy Walker's eyes. Nellie crosses herself again and heaves a heavy sigh.

Aye, Billy Walker, the old man Tulip died and left you high and dry with nowt except the damned old cart shed, he did that. But you brought it on yersel, Billy Walker; yon Billy Walker's only got hissel' to blame.

*

It all happened so quick, Nellie Grainger explains, it was over in a trice, that old cart shed, it went up like a tinderbox, Nellie didn't have time to do nothing. There wouldn't have been no point neither, she says. She'd shouted over the wall, shouted for Billy to get out of the place, knowing all the while it was useless. And him just sat there, Billy Walker just sat there, rocking that damn little babby on his knee and the flames consuming everything and the bairn suck suck sucking at that twisted scrap of butter muslin, Billy never stood a chance. All that stuff he had in there, all them rags and paraffin and them barrels of bones, all gone, gone, all burnt up in less than a minute. And Billy Walker along with it. There was nowt, nowt nobody could have done. Nellie Grainger crosses herself.

As for the bairn, Nellie says, she'd heard it first, she'd heard that self same bairn the night the old man Tulip died; it came with that same wailing. The bairn it came to fetch old Tulip to over yonder. Billy Walker heard it an' all and he went running, running across to the shed, and it was Billy as found the old man lying stone dead on the cart-shed floor.

It's thirty year, Nellie says, thirty year since young Mariah Tulip was delivered of a bonny wee lad and, shortly after, she took the child-bed fever. Hardly more than a bit bairn herself, she'd laboured long and hard to bring that little 'un into the world. Little Billy she named him, against her father's wish. The old man Tulip washed his hands of them, vowed he'd never recognise the bairn, said he'd cast the pair of them out to fend for themselves and sod to Billy Walker. The poor lass was exhausted, too weak even to fight for her own life. Night and day for seven days she burned with the childbed fever, all the while tossing about in the bedclothes and calling out for Billy Walker but the old man wouldn't have Billy darken the door. After seven days we lost young Mariah and her unforgiven body was laid cold to rot in unconsecrated ground. The old man cursed Billy Walker to suffer to the end of his days. And true to his word he took the bairn and the bairn was never seen again. The old man said he'd sent the babby away to be grown up by a wet nurse in a far away place. But Nellie Grainger knows different. Nellie knows what really happened and she'll be silent no longer.

After that day, after what he done, the old Tulip was a broken man, Nellie says. He was never the same again, he was finished, she says, finished. Never once after what he done could he bring himself to light that furnace, not once, not ever again, not after what he done to that babby, poor Billy and Mariah's babby. Every day for the rest of his life old Tulip would go into that cart shed and would throw himself down on his knees in front of that furnace like it was an altar. Every day he begged forgiveness for what he had done but no forgiveness came, not from God on high, nor from Billy Walker. And that carried on, day after day, every day to the day the baby came back, large as life, came back with that self same wailing, came back to claim the old man Tulip and took his life away. And today, it was Billy Walker's turn.

Her tale told, Nellie Grainger sinks back in her chair, she closes her eyes and crosses herself for the last time.

* HARRY'S CAMELLIA *

Every year in April Harry's camellia comes out all pink and blousey. Harry remembers his dear wife Lil. He says planting the camellia was the last thing Lil did before she passed. But it couldn't have been, because there is no last thing.

Did you ever see the film *Lady of the Camellias?* It's about a young woman from the provinces who comes to Paris in search of rising up a rung or two. She too disappears into death but, like Lil, she leaves behind the flowers and the story.

The film is based on the book *La Dame aux Camelias* by Alexandre Dumas, fils, it's just a slim little sliver of a thing but there's nothing flimsy about the story which is fiction but based on the real life of courtesan Marie Duplessis, lover of M. Dumas fils.

I hadn't known there was a Dumas, fils so I investigate. It turns out his great-grandmother was a slave, bought and brought from an unspecified African country to the place now called Haiti. This crucial progenitor is Marie Cesette and she has but a walk-on bit-part in the literary tale.

Marie you are a footnote, a fragment of backstory, a faint shadow in the wings. Heaven only knows what your life was like, what miseries, what struggles you endured, what in the end became of you, what in the final end was your lot, before the possibility of the footnote.

Long long before the bones of the fils were laid to rest in the *Cimetière du Montparnasse*, the bones of Marie Duplessis and the bones of Marie Cesette had been confined in parentheses.

One story conceals another. Marie is a woman of scattered belongings who wades through swamps but the mud never sticks; a strong woman, a woman of courage and heart, a woman who occupies a part of every body called Woman to this day and beyond. Marie never died, she acquired wings; she became a messenger who flies between her world and others, a carrier of tidings across borders, and with those wings Marie can and does travel.

One time she alights in Venice. The year is 1853 and she's flown in to the Teatro La Fenice for the grand world première of *La Traviata*, the opera Verdi has made from Dumas' story of the fallen woman. Soundlessly Marie takes up her place in the Imperial Loggia, she adjusts her fine skirts and sits down. Next to her sits a woman with newer wings, a woman who shares her name and wears, in her hair, the red camellia. Two women from far different and distant times and places sit side-by-side in the theatre box. Holding their opera glasses in place, they watch the movements across the stage.

Their hands touch, their eyes meet, and they know they are part of the same far more ancient story.

Marie, bénie, bénie entre toutes les femmes.

Let no-one say I didn't step into the breach. Our Cara's depressed. I've had to take her in. I said come and stay for a bit, just till you get back on your feet. TLC she needs, that's what everyone says. We could all do with a bit of that eh.

Me and our Cara, we're not actually that close. Back in the day, even then, people said we were chalk and cheese. They'd get our names round the wrong way, or mix the first letter up. They thought it was funny. My sister and me, we used to roll our eyes. As a family, we weren't close either. Everyone scattered hither and thither for various reasons. It did just amount to the proverbial weddings and funerals, and some couldn't be arsed even to manage that. So no, the family wasn't close. Still, you know what they say, blood's blood when all's said and done.

I used to wonder whether blood actually was thicker than water. Because when you think of it, families are where the shit happens. I mean that seriously, you're more likely to be murdered in your family than in some dark alleyway, more likely to be killed by a rello than by a deranged stranger. I mean blood can literally be blood.

Take that family in the flat along our corridor—so-called 'family', I've no idea what they really are. Anyway, them folk along the bottom corridor in our flats. That kid in there, she screams blue murder. Everybody hears it. The Lord only knows what they get up to that makes the kid scream like that, and he's not telling. I've been a bit worried, to be honest, lately, all that racket coming out of there. It could be distracting to my sister for a start, and she doesn't need that kind of stress, not at the moment.

All the same, I'm glad our Cara's here because she needs someone to keep an eye on her medication. People, when they're depressed, you know, either they don't take their tablets–they chuck them down the toilet or out the window or wherever–this is what Dr Gleeson said when he came out that Sunday—or they save the tablets up and take them all at once and bang before you know it they've killed themselves.

When I knew my sister was coming, I took medical advice and the psychi-nurse came over and wrote everything down, all the tablets and all the times and how many such and such and she said she couldn't stress strongly enough how important it was to stick to That regime and to No Other, not to go deviating, however tempting. Anyway, for the sake of clarity, she put it all down in black and white and stuck it up with the fridge magnet.

So I've had my sister sticking to that regime, I've had her sticking to it to the letter, or number rather, you know what I'm saying. I don't let her deviate, even if it means getting her up in the middle of the night and standing over her while she takes the right amount of whatever it is, and I give her a glass of water to wash it down and make sure she swallows it because you know if they're really intent they can hide stuff behind their teeth. So I make her open her mouth wide so I can just check she's not trying anything on because depressed people you know they're like addicts, very expert at deceptions.

They said at first it was that bipolar thing and they asked were there any more in the family, any family history of what used to be called manic depression but isn't any longer. I racked my brains and so did my sister but neither of us could think of anyone. Except, Cara says eventually, what about Granma Baldry. Now when my sister said about Granma Baldry that had me laughing because Granma Baldry wasn't blood was she, or not as far as anyone knows. The psychi-nurse didn't see the funny side. She goes all hoity-toity and she says it's not only blood that gets passed on you know, habits get passed on as well: family secrets can be inherited, every bit as much as your DNA. My sister and me we just look at each other, like what's she on about? We're nearly cracking up, but it's best to let that one pass with only a meaningful look. We burst out laughing though and we laugh and we laugh as soon as the psychi's gone, you should have seen us laughing.

Was she suggesting my sister's extremely debilitating mental condition and total failure to function was nothing more than a habit? A family secret? I seriously hope not. Because anyone can see as clear as day the poor thing is sick from head to toe and there's nothing habit or secret about it.

Anyway, as I say I've been keeping a close eye on my sister and not just as regards the tablets. I've been making sure she eats the right food in the right amounts because they've said it won't hurt to lose a bit of weight. Eat less, move more is what the doctor instructs. I've been meaning to do it with her, that treadmill and that stepping thing at the gym and all, but haven't got it quite organized yet. Up to now I've been mainly watching to make sure she does it properly and she is actually quite adept at it which surprised me. Shedding excess fat, the young woman in the gym says, can give your self-esteem that extra boost. There's loads about it on the net; she showed us how to find it. You can drop a couple of dress sizes in no time. It's really a question of will power. I don't know how much exactly you have to lose before your self-esteem gets high, but anything's better than nothing, that's what I think. It's probably best not to think about it too much though cos thinking makes you feel guilty and then it's a spiral, vicious, downward, all the way to the bottom.

If you ask me—and I've seen this online—a lot of this depression thing is feeling bad about yourself, it's chicken and egg, so anything that makes the feeling-bad thing go away has to be good. So, for that reason I've got our Cara on a strict diet—I'm going to be doing it with her when I get around to it. It's practically raw vegan which I've heard is best for warding off the dreaded diabetes but I've adapted it a bit and managed to incorporate the odd pork chop which she likes as long as it's lean. And you've got to make sure that stuff comes out regular, well, out the other end, because it's no good storing up toxins which can lead to bowel cancer.

This feeling bad thing, I keep on thinking about it and trying to work it out, you can get from your family. Like when they put you down and stuff, it doesn't have to be deliberate, they don't have to mean it. They might even say something as a little joke and not mean you to take offence. I've realised you can make someone feel absolute shit with all the best of intentions. I keep telling my sister nobody means anything nasty. That's how I worry so much about that kid over there, along that corridor, I mean I'm sure her parents are very nice and doing their best and so on, but how's she going to grow up thinking the world is a good place with all that going on in there. That kid'll be ending up like my sister if the situation carries on much longer.

Cara says we should say something and I say like what and she says well it's not normal is it all that screaming and yelling, they must be hurting her, we could tell the doctor or the social services or someone in officialdom, there must be somebody we can tell. So that's what we were talking about the whole of yesterday. But it's not as easy as that is it. I mean you never know what the consequences could be, you never know what can of worms you're opening and it's nothing to do with you.

Those people, that family, they're immigrants of some sort. They could be illegal for all we know. They probably are. You don't want to go dropping them in it. The poor souls have got enough on their plate already without being shopped to the social. And how are we to know what's right when it comes to kids? People make mistakes, otherwise there'd be no need for history, would there. So I said to our Cara, different countries do things in different ways, it's not just a case of when in Rome or right or wrong now is it. It's about Respect and I say that with a capital R. My sister gives me one of her looks and says not if it amounts to 'abuse' you don't; she says that in quotation marks. Of course not. But what goes on behind closed doors.

I don't know what you'd call our childhood for instance. There was no such thing as 'abuse' when we were young.

The NSPCC, my sister says, they took kids away. I remember they did, but there was nothing else was there,
no general awareness, no vigilance, not like now. Marga-
ret Robson's Dad worked for the NSPCC. They lived in a
street perpendicular to ours.

But I can't have my sister going down that road. You
have to watch her. She'll lead you round and round in
circles if she gets half the chance. Argumentative, that's
her way, her way of avoiding things she doesn't want to
look in the face. But as I said to her, be all that abuse
stuff as it may our Cara, it's nothing to do with us in the
here and now; my sole priority is getting you better, and
I said that in italics.

Now, where was I? Yes, to that laudable end—i.e. getting
my sister better—I've worked out a strict regime and a
timetable. She/We have to be able to see an end to all
this malarkey and I don't want this stuff about noisy
neighbours and NSPCCs distracting her from her/our
main task.

Under the nurse's suggestion, I've got her started on
an exercise programme which can do her absolutely no
harm. I'm a great believer—as our old Dad was—in physical
exercise and she will be as well when she sees the results.
Dad used to say a healthy body signifies a healthy mind
and it's a pity my sister didn't pay attention at the time
because if she had she might not have ended up like she
is. Anyway, it's never too late to get started, break the old
habits, remedy the old ways. If she can get a bit of that
weight off to start with, I'll think about taking her down
to the gym and she can meet other people to help her
motivation. But I want to see some reduction in those

flobby bits first. As I said to her, you can't really think Lycra quite at this moment. Give it a couple of weeks, we'll see what happens.

That's why my sister should be focussing on her work-outs and not worrying about those noisy immigrant folk down the way. I went to some trouble–and expense–getting a system organised in the 'spare' room with one of those stepping machines and I intend to see it used. What my sister doesn't appreciate is that people keep themselves to themselves in these flats. It's live and let live, it has to be. It's not the way we do it, spying on people. I haven't got time to be constantly looking out of my peepy-hole.

My sister needs every ounce of encouragement to get going at all never mind the actual exercise she could and should be doing. That's how the depression takes you though isn't it, it makes you drab and weary and lethar-gic to the point of being frankly lazy. Then after that it's downhill all the way, and before you know it there you are, rock bottom, bone idle, not an ounce of your-self left. That's what I keep saying, that's where you're headed, our Cara, if you don't watch out. Regardless of the 'depression'–and I'm saying that in quote marks now because as each day goes by I have more and more ques-tions about what it actually *is*–regardless of her state of mind/mood/inclination my sister has to *get going* and do some exercise before she reaches the stage when what-ever it is gets stuck there for the duration.

Our Cara was very good at swimming, that was her main thing, at school, the thing she was really really good at and no-one else in our family was any good at all so God knows where it came from but she had a definite talent, that's what everybody said. She used to swim for the county. She did think at one point of swimming the channel, that was after she saw *National Velvet* and got inspired by the mother's swimming. She could have done it, easily. I was reminding her about it the other day. I got all the things out, the photographs and the certificates, and I said there you are, they all prove that you are a worthwhile person, blow me down if they don't all prove what a worthwhile person you are, you could have done anything, you're not completely useless like you say and you're not to say things like that any more, do you hear me?

Well first of all she didn't want to look and she pushed the photographs away when I tried to shove them into her hand. I had to make her feel guilty enough so she would look. I said I've spent half the flipping morning sorting through these photographs and laying hands on your certificates which, thank you very much, I have looked after carefully all these years and now you're telling me you're not going to look, well that's ungrateful if ever there was ungrateful! That little speech worked wonders, it fettled her good and proper, and she picked the photos up off the floor one by one and looked. But then she started chucking them aside and she said that none of this and none of that had anything to do with her and I said of course it did, the photographs were living proof of her achievement, incontrovertible, I told her she was in denial, I told her straight, and her denial was just the depression talking, it wasn't really her, it was the depression intent on making her continue to feel worthless because that's what it does, it possesses you like a demon and makes you think the wrong thoughts.

At that point I'm thinking strategically so I go out of the room on the pretext of making us a cup of tea. I leave my sister sitting on the floor surrounded by the photographs and the relics and the certificates. I knew she wouldn't be able to resist picking something up, so I was keep on peeking my head around the door unobtrusively while the kettle was boiling and I was right, she did have a look at the photographs but she quickly put them back down when she heard me coming. But I witnessed something very interesting, which was my sister stuffing one or two up the sleeve of her cardy and I caught that just as I was coming back into the room with the teas.

When I got back into the room my sister seemed to have changed. Something had come over her. I knew this because she then said a very queer thing. Photographs are a queer thing, she said, photographs lie. Which is exactly the opposite of what our old dad used to say. So I said oh no, I said what he said: the camera doesn't lie. The camera can't lie. It's not capable. Those photographs, I said, are proof that you did something to be proud of. She said No Way, very emphatically. They're not proof of anything. Then she said she meant they were not the whole story. Of course not, I said, they're only snapshots. But if you took enough photographs, I said, like every day of your life, every single day, in every situation, you could actually capture the whole story of your life, then the photographs could tell the whole damn story, if you took enough. No you couldn't, my sister said, you could never take enough. I would have argued back but it was then that I saw she'd started crying.

That kid across the way, she mumbled through the tears, there's no pictures of that kid's *real* life is there, no

137

pictures of all that screaming and yelling that goes on all the time now, is there? All that's all missing from the record, wiped off, obliterated; there's no bloody record of the misery now is there and there's never going to be... She was getting herself aeriated so I had to interrupt which is not something I would normally do because I've been advised against it.

Well of course there's no record, I said, you don't take pictures of that sort of thing. You want to take pictures that capture the good things, pictures that remind you of the happy times, not the sad ones. Exactly, family albums are nothing but shit, my sister says, they should be full of all the brutal incidents all the abuse not all the happy fucking clappy. Brutality, she says—she's right on her high horse now—brutality should not be left out of family albums, it should be the stuff of family albums, not conveniently obliterated from the historical record. There should be a law that families are not allowed to peddle their pathetic liar liar stories of happy fucking clappy.

Pure anger had taken over from the crying on my sister's face. I'd been warned about that, about how depression can manifest itself as rage, and produce a peculiar energy, how it could signal the passing into a new phase, how it might be signalling the onset of quite another situation. At that point I thought it best to remove the stimulus so peace could be restored. Keeping as calm and composed as I could manage I got down on my knees and started clearing up the photographs from off the floor and putting them into their packets and packing them neatly back into the box. My sister just sat there watching me and I was almost thinking the rage had subsided but when I came to folding up the certificates she suddenly stretched across and grabbed them out of my hand.

They were hers, she said, and what business did I have hanging onto things that were *hers* and hiding them away from *her* and taking possession of things that were not even mine. Well to say that I was shocked is an understatement because I've always prided myself on being the one to keep the family traditions intact, I've always been the one who looked after those family trinkets and pictures and papers, and no-one could fault me about not looking after them properly or keeping them filed away neatly and in good order. Plus my sister had never once shown any interest in any of that before that moment.

I regret to report that there ensued a bit of a tussle. My sister was intent on wrenching the certificates out of my hand and I was trying to protect them from getting damaged and all I wanted was to get them safely back into the box. My sister behaved like a she-dragon which is what our father always called her, affectionately of course. Well, all in all, I'm sorry to say there was a bit of a fight going on. My sister's accusing me of Christ knows what, I can't even remember the half of it, and there's all this screaming and yelling and my fingernails are clawing into her skin or was it her nails into my skin I don't know which, and handfuls of hair, talk about teeth and claws, the whole situation had got so mixed up and all she wants to do is to grab the certificates and tear them into shreds, and all the while I'm telling myself this is what the depression does to you and it's best if I can try and stay calm until normality can be restored.

But suddenly we're interrupted by this banging on the door and someone's flapping at the letterbox and shouting through the crack. Blow me down if it's not the immigrant man from down the corridor and he's asking is everything alright in there. He's banging on the door and saying do we need help and what's going on and he's tired of all this and he's going to call somebody. My sister and me we compose ourselves very quickly—we're good at that—we smooth down our hair and we put our smiles on, and I open the door and the man's standing there looking very concerned. Is everything alright in there? he says.

It turns out he's not an immigrant after all, he's from Walthamstow. He says he's heard a bit of a commotion and is everything alright. And we say, oh yes fine, everything's fine, we're just watching a video but we've turned it off now and sorry to have disturbed him etc., and he says he's not meaning to be offensive or anything but he's heard noises before coming from my flat and his wife gets a bit nervous with that sort of thing and is there any problem he can help with. And it seems the wife's seen me standing at their door and looking though their spyhole thing and, well, he says I've been standing in the corridor like that for unreasonable amounts of time and making his wife afraid to come out of their flat and she's practically a prisoner in there and it's all because of me and do I have any explanation and he'd be most grateful if we could agree to put an end to it all here and now. Well you could have knocked me over with a feather. A clear case of the pot and the kettle; my sister and I looked knowingly at each other, like we do when we know we are having the same thought.

Naturally I defended myself. I said what can you expect me to behave like, when I'm so concerned about your little girl, I'm on the point of contacting the authorities, I've been so concerned for your little girl, all that screaming and yelling, it sounds to me like she's being half murdered and I've a good mind to report you and it's only out of the goodness of my heart and my concern for you when I thought you were an illegal immigrant and who am I to stand in your way that stopped me but really, I said really, this has gone too far.

Lady, the not-immigrant man interrupts, Lady, he says to me, calm as you like, my dear lady, he says in a loud and slow and exaggerated tone, *we have no child*. You could not have heard any child doing anything in our flat, because *we have no child*, we have *never had any child*, and we do not *anticipate* having a child. So please *please* will you now rest assured we are not abusing or murdering any child in our flat. The crying, the screaming and the yelling, oh yes we've heard it. But lady, lady, it comes from your flat, not from ours.

I felt my sister put her hand onto my wrist, gently, and begin to close the door. Thank you so much, she says to the man, thank you very kindly, we'll be alright now, there won't be any more commotion. She kept her hand on my wrist. I heard her close the door.

It's ok in here, though I'm not so fond of the pale green walls and the food's never any better than lukewarm. My sister's been in to see me twice, and she's coming again on Thursday.

Nobody understood what she was doing. They thought she was throwing food out for the birds, cranky old thing. Some said it would encourage rats, foolish old hag. But, come June, she was surrounded by a whole field of flowers the like of which no-one ever saw. Tourists came and went away with photographs. There's one of her in her red bandana, smiling in the wind, on the cover of Time.

In the summer Sadie had a conservatory built. In the autumn, she moved her desk in there. She was starting a new book, she said, and her study had become stale, stultifying. She put the desk so that it looked out over the garden. Then she moved some books—old favourites, mostly—and lined them up, a small pile at either end to act as bookends.

In the winter, Sadie made some headway with her book. There wasn't really that much of a rush. The important thing was to enjoy, to savour the process, the act of creation. She told Cara this when the branches of the birches were heavy with snow, and she was forever having to fill up the bird feeders. They sat in the conservatory, in basket-work chairs with embroidered cushions, drinking Lapsang Souchong and eating imported strawberries. It was cold, and there was a stony light; they pulled the paraffin stove a little closer.

It was then that Sadie told Cara that the cancer had come back, there were bits of it everywhere, there was no point in any further treatment. She'd come to terms with it, she said.

It'll be all palliative from now on, she said, her voice steady as though guided by some careful tiller.

Cara looked down at the tea steaming in her cup, the slice of lemon floating, stranded. She told Sadie she was sorry; wasn't there something they could do? Surely?

No, don't, Sadie interrupted. There's nothing. It's nothing. She picked up a strawberry and turned it in her fingers, looking at it, before putting it back. I'm resigned to it, really I am, she said.

The bright strawberries looked stupid, pointless in the bowl. A thin drizzle had begun to fall, making tiny pits in the snow. Sadie stood up and pushed back her chair. Cara saw how weary her sister was, how beautiful.

The winter dragged by slowly, as though pulling a heavy weight behind it, though there were some bright days. Sadie and Cara walked in Sadie's garden, the frosted grass still crunchy under the trees where the pale sun never made it. At the pond they poked the thick opaque layer of ice with sticks, trying to free the crinkled leaves embedded there. Sadie talked about her latest book. It was going well, she said.

When the snowdrops came, Sadie could see them from the window, their small heads nodding helplessly in the cold. She sat amongst colourful cushions and blankets and there were always flowers in the vase. She kept her eyes closed a lot.

I'm still waiting for a miracle, she said.

* HOLIDAY TIME *

There comes a time on a holiday when you start count-ing the days in the wrong direction, looking back, turn-ing things over and upside down. Your insides are on the outside and everything's in a muddle, in the wrong place and the wrong way up. But you count on. You carry on ticking off your upside-down calendar, you rip off the pages one by one, you watch each one float away on the smallest of breezes, the briefest of winds.

* THE SPRING AND THE SUMMER
IN NORWAY *

She likes the passing of time, days looming then closing, reaching out ahead with their hands. She likes to see
clouds as they shift across the sky to destinations. She
likes to watch as the sun and the moon half show their
faces together in the night sky that refuses to darken.
She likes it when the spring and the summer in Norway
come so close together, jostling for who can arrive first
and stay longest and the chaffinch and the cuckoo make
alternate calls that carry over the lake and through the
forest, and the lavskrike pairs collect black-beard lichen
for their nests.

She likes it when shadows of birches stretch long across
fields straddling fences at bespoke angles and paces.

She likes the passing of time. All the time she takes
notes of evidence, as this, lest something gets missed
or lost. Things can get lost in the passage of time but
if you're careful you can preserve moments in jars with
formalin words.

I see her look into her cupboard each morning, take
note of its contents, tick, cross, label, list, enumerate. I
see she likes it when things get used up, have reached the
end of their natural life; jars of jam, pickles, preserves;
fresh vegetables that have begun to pucker and bend,
about to set off in new directions; delicacies of long forgotten origin. She ticks off each thing and marks them
Discard and Replace but it's an act of verbosity only, for
the items remain.

I see her line up her creams and her lotions on the
shelf in the bathroom. She has a system there too and

there's real delight on her face when she's squeezed the last drop of something and she can put its tube or its carton into the Finished box which grows and grows.

In all these ways she reveres the passing of time. It acts to remind her she's alive and counting.

* LAUNDRY AT 904 MOH *

Your clothes are hanging out there on the line, hand-washed, still dripping. The sun has not yet arrived where they are hanging but it will come and your clothes will be dry. You like to see this line of garments that belong to you, and only you, arranged sentry before your window. They stand guard of who you are, they remind you each time your mind wanders off alone across the blue lake and along the winding path on the other side, wanders off among the dark firs and through the dark forest and up and up past Grassli-sæter and up some more to nearly the top of the mountain when you pass the tree line and go beyond where the snow still lies.

Note: Fefor, in Nord-Fron, Norway, where this was written, is 904m above sea level.

In a strange variation on the Dorian Gray theme one side of her face aged whilst the other didn't. The progression was slow—as is the case with ageing—but there came a moment when the differentiation of the two sides, if not complete, was evident. She'd peer into the mirror, apply ointments, count lines, measure fissures, monitor hair follicles minutely as the eyebrow on one side receded into nothingness.

Surveying the differential impact of the years became a time-consuming occupation, there was no time for anything else; other aspects of her life and her self, the workplace, the home environment, the therapy—all were neglected, then foregone. She could always catch up she could always catch up but she couldn't and wouldn't and she didn't, and in this way the years ran away with more than one side of her face.

The years, that day, were seen running down the road, hurrying along the High Street, past the Hotel and the Post Office and the doctor's surgery and that place where you used to be able to book holidays. They were spotted hurtling at great speed past the garage by Willy the garage man who stood looking on incredulous; he lifted his oily Tom Paxton cap with one hand and scratched his head with the other. The years were no sooner come than they'd gone, Willy would later recall; flown past, and away. And they were carrying not only half that woman's face—which side it was, the garage man couldn't rightly say—but were also dragging behind them on a long long rope everything she had ever had or been or owned or desired. Yes, the years ran away with every damn thing, that's how it was, the garage man said.

* A BRIEF BIOGRAPHY *
For Andrew

A man in a pale green smock cut you from your mother's body with a slicing knife. He was flailing as much as you were. He put his shiny instruments into the boiler to wash all trace of you away. He rinsed his hands. He looked across the pale green room in the pale green light; he looked at your mother whose hair was damp, whose eyes were closed. Someone came and stitched up the gaping bloody hole in your mother's belly where they had pulled you out. You started screaming. It was the first sound you ever heard, and you didn't know what it was.

Your father wore a suit, a tweed suit, of a pale green colour, made in Ireland, after the moss that coats the damp peat by the sides of the sheep tracks. The weave was rough against your smooth face. Your father had money in his pocket; you heard it rattle. He looked down at you with eyes the colour of walls. Your eyes, squinting, tiny, did not yet focus. You had no idea who he was, that man with the rough green skin and the walls for eyes.

Now that you had come, your father was thinking of Norway. He was thinking of Gålå, of the red wooden *hytte* in the wild green *kve* where the globe-flowers and the harebells and the *tyttebær* toss their girly heads in the fine warm grass. It was August. All down the side of the mountain, all the way down to the Gålåvatn, the fir trees stirred, the scent of resin drifted on the air. Across the lake, in the distance, snow-capped mountains rose blue in the haze. Your father will take you there when the time comes.

You are a child in a portrait painted by an itinerant Spanish artist. You hang opposite your brother on the cold wall of the drawing room where no-one ever goes. Your mother is in the blue-painted kitchen, making ginger granthams. She beats butter and sugar in the Mason's bowl until her arm is tired. She looks out into the Hampshire afternoon and thinks of Blackloch, of the small white painted house reflected in the water where the otters dive. She smells bluebells and daffodils, wild garlic in the Galloway woods; she worries about the encroachment of rhododendrons and caravans. There's a little boat tied up at the jetty, bobbing gently in the water, in the wispy shadows of the trees.

They send you away to school because that is what they do and they do it. They spend a long time choosing, a good one that will make you into a fine young man. They dream for you: a lawyer, perhaps, or a churchman, like your godfather in Bridge of Allan, or an Officer, like your mother's brother whose name you should be honoured to bear; the uncle you never knew who no longer needs his name. The school makes you tired and angry, but that's how things are. Matron is kind and her skirts are warm and in the summer you lie on the playing field and watch the cricket and you eat the ginger granthams your mother sends wrapped in greaseproof paper.

Oh look, here come the horses, your father's passion. In the holidays you ride up onto the hill in the early mornings. You hear the metallic squawk of the pheasant as it flaps about in the corn stubble, too heavy to lift off without an effort. Your father takes snuff and issues commands and sometimes he makes you laugh. In the winter, you ride to hounds and they smear fox blood on your face and present you with a severed tail. Your mother puts her hand on your head, but says nothing.

You eat your ice cream alone in the dining room. Above the door, in the hallway, the fox's head still hangs, its yellow teeth bared.

With your father you walk for days in the Jotunheimen, looking out towards a vast expanse of sky; you're up beyond the tree line, way beyond the fir trees and the spruce and the tight dry heather and the twisted stubbled birch. The air is light and this is the only place on earth you can breathe with any ease. In the wide green valley far below sheep tear rhythmically at the close-cropped turf, the muffled clank and echo of their neck-bells the only sound. Poetry comes to you easily but you tell no-one. Your father makes bloody plans for catching trout; you will help him put the nets out at Little Jetningen, you will help him pull them in, you will help slash the slithering fish open and scrape the purpling guts into the chipped enamel pail that stands outside and attracts flies. Your mother never comes to Norway and you do not miss her.

Alternate years, you go to Galloway. You row the little boat out on the Blackloch, your arms are growing strong. Your mother, sitting in the bow, points out a heron standing sentry among the rocks. Gulls wheel and screech overhead and the water is getting choppy. Your oars dip rhythmically as you bend and pull, bend and pull, glancing over your shoulder to line up the jetty. You help your mother out of the boat, and you notice how cold her hands are, how papery the skin. You are young and strong and she is old. She smiles, gathers up her skirt and begins the short climb up the hill. The dachshunds run and leap, yapping on the grassy bank, worrying shadows, as you tie the boat up with the proper knot.

Your mother takes you to Lochnaw, to the crumbling grey castle where she was born. The cold stone kitchen smells of ancestors, and thick brown tea is poured into chipped china cups. You eat shortbread and fruitcake and the sound of the wind is hollow in the chimney. This is where your middle name comes from. You read it under the portraits, you read it on the crest.

One time, you walk alone along the cliffs, all the way from Dunskey to Killantringan. You stand for a long time looking over at the House of Knock, a big white house that sits on the edge and looks out across the Irish Sea.

Your mother, as a child, in skirts and a clean white pinafore, thick stockings and little black boots, is by herself down there on the shore, collecting shells and putting them into her pocket that is already bulging. How tiny she looks down there on the shoreline, how far away. She does not yet know that her mother will die, that her brothers will die, that she will marry your father, that you will put her ashes to rest forever in this place. For now, just for now, she's a child, just a child, engrossed in collecting shells.

You walk back up the steep muddy track towards the road where you left the car. The wind blows in from the west, a sticky salty feel to it. Behind you, the waves crash on the rocks and froth and foam in all the little crevices before pulling back to gather up strength again.

Your ancestors are open mouths still waiting to be fed long after their portraits have slipped in the gallery, fought shy of their frames, curled up at the edges and faded, faded.

In the family gallery the nails that hold up the hanging frames have rusted. All the way up and up the wide staircase up and up to the very top the cobwebbed images of ancestral glories tilt and skew, foxed and cracking and peeling.

Your kids will, in their turn, climb staircases, ride mountains, carry backpacks stuffed full to overflowing with what you have left and not left, with what you have said and not said.

My counsel: bequeath only the capacity to recognise baggage and instructions on how not to trip over it lest it break your bones.

Now, picture your kids with their backpacks on, picture them trudging up one hill after another and the hills are getting higher. What have they got stuffed in that luggage there, for god's sake? What's that, bulging out? What are all those things suspended on the outside, hanging and dangling and clanking about on ropes and strings and chains? And what's that they've got trailing? Looks like entrails, dragging along and picking up dirt; what are they doing with entrails?

Wheels of course could make the entire enterprise easier. Did you leave them some wheels? Or are your kids going to have to invent their own?

My counsel: Leave your kids with only enough stuff to make a picnic, which should include wheels.

Long long ago, in the thick dark forest that covers the steep rocky slope on the edge of the village of Rørholt in Telemark, there stood a small wooden house by the name of *Svarverkjær*. The forest, with its trees of spruce and pine, larch and birch and rowan; its undergrowth of juniper, so sweetly scented; its summer edges of harebells, raspberries, heather and fine fine grasses, and ferns as bright and fresh and green as you have seen; or its autumn clumps of *blåbær* and *tyttebær* and a hundred different kinds of mushroom—this forest was home to *Svarverkjær* and the forest kept the house safe and that's how things were and that's how they had always been.

The little wooden house had been made many years ago by an old old man, a man who had always been old and who would always be old, a man who lived all his long long life in the forest. He worked with the trees and he made his living from the trees and the trees, in their turn, were kind to him and allowed him to fashion out of them such lovely things, and one of those lovely things was the little wooden house which was his home and which he painted white and which he named *Svarverkjær*.

The old man was also a highly skilled hunter, for there were many creatures in the forest. He hunted bears and he hunted wolves, and deer of several different types, and he hunted wolverine, and he hunted musk ox. The old man knew how to stalk and to trap and to catch and to kill; he knew how to prepare and to cure and preserve the skins and the horns and the meat and the feet and the bones so that not a bit of the animal went to waste. And in this way the old man lived at *Svarverkjær* and made his living from the forest.

When the time came for the old man to stop being old, he went away; he went away and he left the little white house standing alone on the rocky hill in the forest where it had always stood.

Very soon after the old man had gone, the forest trees realised that a new freedom was theirs and they determined to take advantage of it. They allowed their young to take root willy-nilly all over the place and get into tangles. The cherry trees delighted in dropping their fruit anywhere and everywhere across the once proud grassy paddock. The ash trees grew far bigger than they ought and dared creep closer in, bending and stooping and tap tap tapping their thinnest branches at the cobwebbed glass of the little windows and peering in.

The stream that once trickled so sedately down the sloping kve from the deep dark well began to gush noisily, this way and that, any way it pleased, and at times decided to cease its gush altogether and make the well dry. The pond allowed its water to rise and fall without reason or warning; it invited so many rushes to live round its edges, and ferns, and even some wild roses, and sometimes you couldn't see its water at all. Ditches clogged themselves up with mud and with silt; fallen stones fell in and couldn't get back out, causing floods every time the rains came. And the track that leads up from the Tokevann to Svarverkjær all but disappeared under determined wiry grasses and sedges in the damper places. This is what happened after the old man went away and all these things made Svarverkjær feel quite gloomy.

But as the years passed, Svarverkjær survived and he learned to live by himself, he learned a new contentment in the movement of the seasons, he came to understand how new things come along to take the place of the old. Each year he noticed something new going awry, but he also observed how new solutions appeared, as if by miracle, as if by magic. One year, for example, when his chimney stack crumbled with the weight of the snow and the ice sneaking into the finest of cracks and fracturing them open, no sooner had the chimney stack fallen than a pair of hooded crows moved in and made the ruin their home. They piled their nest high with twigs and sticks and pieces of bracken and kept themselves safe in the old chimney to raise a family of four.

It has been a long hot summer. And still, so still, the air so still, as though time himself had stopped to ponder; everything so very still, through the months of long warm days that stretched into nights and nothing moved. Now it's autumn, and the sun crosses the sky lower down and more quickly, spreading her evening pink across the *Tokevann*, she watches the dew gather on the tips of the grass, she follows the shadows as they climb up the bumpy track and into the woods and up to the pond and beyond until there are shadows all around the house of *Svarverkjær*. The autumn mornings are softened by an early mist that rises as the warmth of the earth and water meets cooler descending air. When the sun nudges the tops of the tallest pines over there in the distance, the mist will retreat and wait for its turn again in the morning.

It is late September. A bee buzzes about its business, anxious to get finished before the long cold spell arrives and makes everything sharp. A chaffinch chirrups in the cherry tree. Rivalrous blackbirds keek keek keek at each other under the apple trees, each trying to get at the best of the pickings. A pair of magpies struts along the ridge of the old red barn. In the woods, a jay watches; a woodpecker hammers, demanding insects. A buzzard circles on currents high above the wild rocks at the top on the mountain, and mews. Svarverkjær listens, hears the mice scratching among his rafters, scuttling busy inside his walls; they too are fetching and carrying their stores for the winter. Bats, lined up in the loft, hang upside down, waiting for dusk and moths.

Dusk, in the autumn: this is the time when the sun settles down behind the shadows, the time when the Elk will come. The Elk will come to the orchard to enjoy the apples that drop from the trees and which no-one picks, not any more, not since the old man went away. As the sun edges down behind the tall birches that stand on the hill to the west, Svarverkjær watches and waits anxiously for the Elk. A great lumbering animal, the Elk will nevertheless manage to arrive in silence. He'll stop by the pond and lift his great head, he'll sniff the air before bending to take a long drink of the cool clear water.

Svarverkjær, waiting, must have dozed—he's getting old, more easily tired—and dusk is already closing in when he wakes to the sound of the cracking of twigs and the soft thud thud of apples dropping to the grass. He knows at once that the Elk had arrived. Svarverkjær looks out over the orchard, sees the Elk reaching up into the branches of the furthest tree with his great head, watches how he takes one old bough after another in his soft mouth and moves it lazily this way and that until, one after another, the ripened apples fall to the ground. The house watches as the Elk nudges his nose among the fallen apples, selects a good one and eats, his jaw moving from side to side as he chews. Svarverkjær watches for more than an hour as the Elk eats the apples one by one.

The Elk was late coming this year, later than usual, and Svarverkjær had worried he would not come at all. Then, when he finally arrived, it seemed to Svarverkjær that the Elk moved more slowly, that his gait was a little more stooped, his steps less certain. An outsider would see an elk, a plain old elk, a large one to be sure, male, getting on in years, his seniority indicated by the ten pointed antlers proudly displayed on a head held high. But to Svarverkjær, who had watched and who had waited and who knew how everything has been and how it should be, the change in the Elk stirred something inside him, gave rise to thoughts in his bowel that would not go away.

He's like me, Svarverkjær thought, we're one of a kind, we're getting old. The old Elk is slowing up, as sure as the autumn slows everything up, as sure as all of us gather ourselves up for the long cold winter.

And yet it seemed to Svarverkjær to have been not so very long ago when the Elk had been in his prime: brave and proud and strong, he'd stood two meters to the shoulder, he'd moved through the forest with a power, with a certainty of his high head, he'd stepped out with the confidence of an undisputed ruler. And he'd bellowed, how that Elk had bellowed! Svarverkjær can almost hear it from across the years, that bellow, the depth of it, the resonance, the message it carried right across the forest: this Elk is the King around these parts and he intends for things to stay that way. And Svarverkjær didn't mind admitting how he himself had swelled with pride to hear the Elk–his Elk–claiming rulership of the forest at the very peak of his greatness; yes, all that, not so very long ago.

But greatness, thinks Svarverkjær, greatness is a passing

state that one day will lose its significance and, at that stage, will readily be handed on.

And indeed the Elk had fathered many wild keen youngsters who now roamed the forest and who, each year, grew more proud, more strong; and all were looking to take their places, ready to fight for the top position.

Svarverkjær is still watching the Elk in the orchard as darkness closes in.

Yes, he is thinking, time moves on, and time moves us on. We must move with it or be left behind.

Svarverkjær's roof creaked agreement; his walls creaked too, and the mice shuffled under his floorboards. In the darkness, the trees in the forest swayed and whispered.

Everything changes, thought Svarverkjær, it all changes as surely as the clouds dash across the sky in the autumn winds, as surely as the sun hides herself behind them, as surely as the moon rises and swells in the winter darkness and stills the long nights into silence.

This year, the apple crop had not been so good. As can be the way with apples, one tree had not produced any fruit at all but had remained defiantly barren, a warning that the winter would be a harsh one. The Elk would need as much food as he could get to keep him strong for the time when the bleak winds blow in from the north and the big snows arrive and settle for months on end, covering all the trees and making their branches dip, coating the ground and freezing up the Tokevann. The days would soon be very short, the nights long and so very cold.

Yes, the Elk needed to build up all his strength for the winter which would come soon enough, Svarverkjær knew. The winter would come quickly on the tails of the first frost that would change the colours of the birches, rowan and ash completely and make their leaves rustle and fall. The light would change and the sky would change and the trees would sway and lash and their leaves come landing damp and brown to the earth till the branches were stripped bare enough to resist the winter.

It pleased *Svarverkjær* to watch the plants and the birds and the animals around him preparing for the winter. The leaves of the *blåbær* reddened, and those of the shy tiny *tyttebær* smiled up before they thinned and fell; the heather too, its purple flowers curled dry and brown, hugged itself closer to the earth for shelter. The mushrooms took their final chance and swelled quick and huge, ripening proudly for the last time before their underground retreat from the dark cold months. The woodland creatures, the voles and the mice and the weasel, the polecat and the little red squirrel worked night and day with the help of the *Nisser* to gather up stores to last them through the snow-time. Toads and frogs and newts and salamanders crawled out from their watery homes and made for sheltered places in soft moss, among stones, piles of warm leaves and under fallen logs on the forest's edge.

Svarverkjær watched all these creatures; they knew what they were doing, he knew they would cope with the winter. Big forest owls screeched when darkness came; they too knew how to look after themselves. Many of the smaller birds had gathered themselves into flocks a month ago and made off to warmer places where they would stay until the snows melted at *Svarverkjær* and spring came once again. All these plants and animals knew how to look after themselves. It was only the Elk that *Svarverkjær* was worried about.

Darkness had long closed in but Svarverkjær was unable to rest. High winds from the North were beginning to bring icy cold; he tensed as they blew angrily round his walls, as they battled round and round, seemingly determined to get in. Svarverkjær's walls shuddered as they resisted, they groaned their warnings for the wind to come no closer. But Svarverkjær knew nothing could withstand the real onslaught of winter and the great blasts of frozen air that would chill him to the core. He could rattle and shake his windows and his walls all he liked in protest, but to no avail; the wind was relentless. Winter was almost on the doorstep. The mice scampered and scratched to hide themselves in warmer places.

Wide-awake that long cold night, Svarverkjær knew the Elk had not gone back to the forest to sleep after his feed as he should have done. He had not returned to his mossy bed among the sweet smelling juniper; he was still out there, in the orchard, where he'd been since dusk. He'll be freezing, thought Svarverkjær, freezing out there, in the orchard, standing by himself, in this wind.

But Svarverkjær had no way of helping the Elk. All he could do was to wait anxiously for dawn to open the dark into lightness so he could see across to the orchard and observe the Elk and make sure everything was alright. But the winter nights in Rørholt are long and they don't easily give up their thick black cloaks. Svarverkjær waited anxiously for dawn to show her pale face.

As dawn drew closer, Svarverkjær could just make out the Elk still standing under the apple trees. But the Elk was not at rest, he kept twisting round, nudging at his flank with his nose, and he wasn't taking any of his weight on his leg on that side. Observing this, Svarverkjær knew that the Elk had been injured; there'd been a fight and he'd suffered an injury. He's been replaced, Svarverkjær knew at once; this is what happens. There's been a fight and a younger contender has taken over the top position in the forest. There's no future for this Elk, thought Svarverkjær sadly. The only future for this Elk is at the end of the barrel of a hunter's gun, his head and his fine fine antlers will go for a hunter's trophy.

Svarverkjær could hardly bear the thought of it, the thought that his magnificent Elk would end his days as hunter's meat, tracked down and chased through the forest, the very thought of it made Svarverkjær quake with grief and anger.

Svarverkjær had known this Elk for many years, for as many years as the Elk had been coming to Svarverkjær. The Elk and the little house had known and watched each other since the Elk was just a calf, a little suckling calf with big floppy ears and a hopeful face. He'd come with his mother, wobbling along on his gangly legs, up the track to Svarverkjær, to visit the old man. True, the old man had been a hunter, a hunter through and through, but for a reason he'd always kept to himself, the old man had made an exception for this Elk; this Elk was different: this Elk was not to be harmed, he was never to be harmed.

So Svarverkjær had watched the Elk as he grew up, had seen him as he ambled beside his mother as a cheeky yearling, then as a youngster, already showing early signs of the magnificent beast he would become. His mother brought him to drink at the pool. It was his mother who'd taken him to the orchard and, with the old man's blessing, had shown him the apples, taught him how to shake the branches to topple the ripe ones which were the best to eat.

Yes, this Elk had been the old man's Elk, and now he was going to be hunter's meat and Svarverkjær couldn't stand it. October, and the forests of Bamble Kommune are alive with hunters and Svarverkjær knows his Elk is in danger. And he knows the Elk, with his injured flank, will never be able to escape the long sure sight of a keen hunter's gun.

Dawn breaks, misty and cold as the pale sun struggles to see through the cloud. The Elk is still resting under the apple trees, the bleeding wound on his flank now clearly visible. And in the distance, Svarverkjær hears the voices and the steps and the baying of the dogs of the hunters as they make their way up the forest track.

Surely, he thinks, surely, the Elk hears them too, surely he smells the smell of death from the deer they'll be carrying over their shoulders, surely he'll sense the presence of the elkhounds whose job it is to locate their quarry and to chase them into clearings where they're visible enough for the hunters to take aim and to shoot. Surely he'll know he's in danger, he'll run away…

But no, as Svarverkjær watches, the Elk continues to stand in the orchard, his head hung low; perhaps, thinks Svarverkjær, perhaps the Elk doesn't realise the danger he is in; perhaps he's too old and too sick to move.

The hunters and their dogs advance up the hill. Svarverkjær hears them talking and laughing, hears the elkhounds panting as they scuffle and scurry about in the undergrowth.

Svarverkjær braces himself and he clenches himself and he twists himself; he wills his every last ounce of strength to twist himself so that his walls creak and they groan and they creak some more and they twist and they bulge and eventually they begin to shift.

The poor walls have no idea what Svarverkjær is doing, twisting them about like that. Terrified of falling down, the walls are determined to stand their ground. They demand to know what in the Great Forest's name Svarverkjær thinks he is doing, why is he twisting them like that; is he seriously attempting to put them all out of shape, so they will all collapse? so they could never again be mended? Does he not realize he's putting their very lives in danger?

But Svarverkjær knows, and he knows very well, that a house cannot stand without walls, or not for long.

Stop it now! Stop what you're doing! the walls all plead in their loudest creaking voices.

But Svarverkjær is looking only at the Elk, watching him still standing there in the orchard. The house braces himself ever more strongly, and twists, he heaves and twists himself until his north wall begins to crack, and he twists some more until it crumples and he twists some more until finally it gives way and falls to the ground, shattered in pieces.

His mission achieved, Svarverkjær stands still and waits. The Elk can come now and find shelter in Svarverkjær's collapsed north wall. Surely he'll come, the Elk will come and find refuge there. But as Svarverkjær watches, still the Elk stands unmoving in the orchard as the hunters draw ever closer.

The hunters and their dogs are coming round the corner now by the big red barn, their breath before them in clouds in the early morning air. Svarverkjær knows his one last chance of saving the Elk has been lost.

But just as he gives up his very last hope, Svarverkjær sees something strange, something very strange is happening in front of him. Is that the old man he sees, leading the Elk across the track, coming towards Svarverkjær and guiding the injured animal to the side of the house that has crumbled.

If you go now to *Svarverkjær*, you'll see the little wooden house still stands at the top of the forest track, as it always did. You'll see the north wall has been mended and new people are living there. Children play by the pond and have made swings in the orchard; they're growing up to know elks and to love them and to share with them the apples in the orchard. The children will tell you how, every year, as autumn turns to winter, an old man comes, a very old man, he comes to the orchard, and he brings with him an Elk, and he sits and he watches as the Elk eats his fill of the fallen apples. Then, the two of them, they go away again, they disappear into the forest together, as darkness closes in and winter comes once more.

I see Patti Smith waving from the window of the Rimbaud house. She's looking out of the open window past the peeling faded green shutters and across the garden all overgrown. There are bars on the windows of the ground floor rooms.

This is the place—the very room I believe—near Charleville where the great poet wrote his major work *Une Saison en Enfer*. The year was 1863 and it is said he never wrote a single poem after he reached the age of twenty-one, not one.

I have now reached the age of sixty-five and the year is 2018. I have not hitherto studied Rimbaud but I believe I'm going to now.

I've known for a long time how much he was revered by people at whose feet I myself have fallen—Dylan, Kerouac, the Beats, Patti Smith; they were all onto Rimbaud and for years I've found their reverence terrifying.

It's not that I'm afraid of reverence or intensity. I can take both. The fear is that if I look Rimbaud in the face I will see nothing and it will be my fault, purely my own fault. It will be my own failing because I can't stand the chaos there must have been in his head and how he kept moving and living in different places and getting shot by his friend and not remembering anything and I can't stand any of that. And an added extra trouble is that I know, I actually know how it is that one poet could shoot another poet; I actually understand how that could happen.

I would however like to visit his house, I'd like to be quiet there, I'd like to just be quiet there and be at his house and look out of that window.

Next to me your new grey suitcase waits, the name-tag says you belong here at Lomsetervegen, 5.

For now, this is home—as home as home would be—where I sit on reindeer hide in a cabin made of wood, where we burn birch on the *peis* in the *stue*, catching the smell.

All around there is silence, day and night, night and day, silence. And the lake is still and eternal, and the mountains are still and eternal—as eternal as eternal would be—and the sky only ever gets whiter. Even at night, especially at night, the sky gets ever whiter.

And A. has just phoned from Vinstra station, not a soul about, he says. And ditto ditto I say from here.

I stand at the door of an airless room that smells of wood and sleep. The bed—two duvets, two pillows, side by side—ritualistically done and undone. The duvets are naked.

There's comfort in patterns that recur and repeat to provide shelter—hiding places, cages with or without bars, places for rest that allow you to shelter to hide in a hollow and to rest when they're in place all in place.

I sit on the reindeer skin chair in the *stue*. The stove in the kitchen is lit but needs watching. It needs watching and tending if you're going for warmth.

I will go for a walk along to the *bom* and back, you can manage that. The resident *røyskatt* is doing his house-work. Later you can clear up and get on with *Devotion*. Outside, the wind in the Scots' pines and a grey cloud coming over to shadow some part of this vista before it moves on.

I will keep the stove in the kitchen going with the birch you cut with your axe before you sliced into your leg. I will find my glasses, do some laundry.

She bought it for her honeymoon, your mother did. The blue faux leather won't crack, the shop woman reassures. Muriel, not understanding faux, buys the case and believes it to be real leather all her life, the faux so easily transformed by dreams.

When dreams get in the way, that's ok, her father says, closing the door behind him. Ruby scowls into the steaming broth on the stove that's never hot enough.

A small blue suitcase in which your mother packed every damn dream she could think of, she stuffed it full and off she went to the Isle of Skye. It was the end of summer, and the year was 1952.

Now people have said many times to me, 'What did Stella have in that case, what did she have packed in there?' And I change my mind all the time. Today, I say, she had her dreams in there, her notebook and her dreams and a brush for her wild red hair.

I like it when my small suitcase has just enough in it; essentials, things I can rely on; things counted out, ticked off. I lay the things out side-by-side, all fit perfectly into their own spaces.

See how they lie there, waiting. See how they're all so patient, ready, willing, waiting. And look at Pink Monkey, keeping guard.

I like to pack Pink Monkey and seven of everything. Black pants, black socks, tee-shirts (mostly black). One jacket (black, wearing). One pair of dungarees (dark green, wearing), 3 pairs of Lucy+Zac cotton trousers, a thin jumper, a thicker jumper, my soap things. Technological aids (laptop + chargers, etc.). Notebook, pens and pencils, sharpener. That's it.

Only then is it safe to move in any direction.

However long I'm away, I will need 2–3 books. The rest I have to read on the Kindle app and hurt my eyes. It has to be this way if I am intent on travelling light which I am. I don't wish to lug unnecessary baggage at any time or for any distance or at any stage of my life, not any more.

Unnecessary baggage can come from the past, the present, or the future and needs weeding out, continual weeding out is required to keep on top of unnecessary baggage.

See me perched precarious on a baggage-summit, I am a body-cairn atop a baggage-mountain of unnecessary that has piled up under me in the few hours I stopped weeding. And the nights are chilly up there high on that baggage-peak.

And once again the bag is packed; there, on the floor, it gapes its wound, its innards spilling out. Or vulval, its private parts exposed to my current indecision.

I will not close it, not just now. I will not fasten its contents in. I cannot zip it closed, not yet. I hear its silence say j'accuse j'accuse.

A rolled up teeshirt lies dormant waiting. The sponge bag caught beneath the net—these days when nobody has time for sponges.

The suitcase waits. Its last Air France flight tag grubby but still attractive still hanging on recalls some previous journey that turned out here right here like this.

Don't look at me like that, don't you judge me.

So what, if putting on this face is a thing I need to do, a ritual that has to be observed before I can dare brave the day or dare anything. So what. Don't judge me.

So what if crouching here is what I do. Don't judge me.

So what if I am lying down. So what if I look like this. So what if I am from where I am. You stand in my shoes before you judge me.

You crouch in my shoes before you judge me.

You stand in my shoes for 65 years and if you make it that far that's when you can judge me.

But in 65 years or 65 miles or 65 minutes having different shoes on your feet means your feet will no longer belong on your legs. When you look down you will see your feet are different feet, new feet, walking a path you didn't know; new feet, new path, will carry you forward to somewhere else.

The woman in the mirror turns and you notice the eyes in the back of her head.

I can read you like a book, she says, like a book with these eyes in the back of my head.

In Norway we measure a *gapahuk* for size and shape, take photos of its precise construction, think about possible locations for the fire; we have a corner fire, its shape conditions its position.

This *gapahuk* sits at the foot of the ski-lift at Feforkampen, right by the path where, as a child, you came running down the grassy bank between the trees, holding on tight to the little troll you'd found in the rocks by the Feforvann. Down the rough track you hurdled, running so fast over the bumps I feared you'd trip over or tip forward or, for some other reason, fall. But you knew everything then, you'd already found out the important things. You'd steered your course. You'd keep on holding on.

I look now out across that same green *fjell*; how the grasses move in the wind, and a few slow sheep with their bells graze safe in the shadow of the summer *hytte*. I look out across to Fagerli and the fields cleared of trees around Grassli-sæter, and my eyes turn then towards the sky where white puffs of cloud shift west to east, how they chase and swell and merge all into each other.

Note: A gapahuk is a three-sided mountain or woodland shelter.

* who's speaking through your mouth *

I read a lot. I think of other writers and how I can learn from them. Every day it seems I learn something from Patti Smith. Not just simple 'wisdoms,' though there are those, and not just the ability/necessity to see to the heart of things and how what matters matters and has to matter. But this one-sided connection I have with Patti Smith seems to allow some of her wisdoms and some of her process/method to rub off on me, not in terms of actual thoughts and revelations but more in terms of process and how I find myself thinking about things, coming at things with a new tilt, *thinking beyond my own thoughts*, like you begin to do in therapy. You think a thing or you feel a thing and you've barely registered what it is when right on its heels comes another very different thought that pushes the first thought out the way and the second thought that comes, the one that supervenes, is a *guiding thought*, it's not an ordinary thought, it's a kind of *tiller*, or a *steering thought*, like it's come in new from the outside and is now working on the inside and it's showing you another way, another path, one which is a bit different from where you were headed or thought you were headed, but this is a different way, a new way, and why not try it just give it a go and before you can even make that decision the words are out of your mouth and you have actually put a foot down on that new road and you're thinking hey, who's that speaking through my mouth?

So there you are, you allow yourself to be introduced to the new path, like in Robert Frost's *The Road not Taken*, and you realise what's happening is some kind of *transformation of trust*, something of it is *taking root* inside you and there you are, allowing yourself to hold someone's hand and you wonder if this is what it's like to have a mother.

* FEFOR *

I walk out with my notebook just in case. I don't dare walk far. Don't ask. I don't need a map.

I walk alongside pines and birches and spruce. There's a warm wind today that makes the trees talk and give out small resinous smells. The sky is blue and white in equal amounts. Shadows of trees move a little on the grey *grus* road. I see signs of sheep, a *lavskrike*, a magpie. I don't forget the mantra, not like my mother forgot the mantra. I will never ever forget the mantra.

In the far west, the Jotunheimen, still snowed, still glaciered, in today's bright light, presiding.

A woodpecker hammers his hope on a dead tree somewhere close by. The gate at the cattle bridge creaks. The ground here is strewn with fir cones; at night, if there's wind, you hear them bang bang bang on the roof. The wildflower verges now are at their best. I try to capture some ground in an iPhone photo but I can't. So much is missing. So much that is there but isn't.

She lifted the wooden statue down, carefully dislodging the nails. The removal left the pale space of a man on the door stained thick with age. She carried the statue home and with the long dark braids of her hair she anointed the feet. Then she lay down with him for two days and two nights and on the third day she died. A four-sided nail was found clasped in her cold hand. I prefer to lie among the wooden dead, she said. That night the robed figure of a man was seen making his unsteady way down the road. By morning a carved wooden statue hung again on the door, a woman this time.

Note: The carved wooden statue that hangs on the door of the church is thought to be the tax collector or customs officer Sakkius, or Zacchaeus, whom Christ is said to have brought down from the sycamore tree symbolizing the official's turn to humility. Some identify Zacchaeus with the apostle Matthew. Above the statue on the door are inscribed the words in old Norwegian Den bod far dige tolder, for which no precise translation is available but which refers to repentance for all things taken for one's own gain.

* SAINT CUTHBERT *

You hadn't remembered you'd made a bookmark out of Saint Cuthbert and you'd taken the book on holiday—you always like to re-read on holiday because a different time a different place makes the words entirely new. Saint Cuthbert parted company with The Good Soldier and fell to the floor in the wooden cabin you'd rented in the mountains for solitude. And when you stooped to pick up the picture your fingers reached out to trace the knots in the wood that looked like eyes and your knees were on the floor.

Jim thinks he's dead.

Do you mean deaf?

No, Jim thinks he's dead.

Is it himself or another person who Jim thinks is dead?

No Jim. He thinks he's dead.

How can he be dead?

I don't know. I suppose he died.

How did he die? You can't just die.

I don't know. I just know Jim thinks he's dead.

Well tell him he's alive. Tell him he must be alive or he couldn't think he was dead or think anything else. Tell him.

I did. But he just keeps saying he's dead.

He must mean it metaphorically. That he's dead inside. Or numbed of feeling. Has he suffered a trauma?

Yes. He died. He is dead.

That summer we lived in the little wooden *hytte* half way up the mountain at Fefor. There were some endless days. They moved and we moved slowly, as though hypnotised, or under some divine instruction. We lived amidst wood. Birches, spruce and Scots pine mainly, the towering ones. Then there were dwarf willow, birches, juniper, and *blåbaer* all over, all keeping ground. The little *lafthus*, the walls and the floors and everything built inside and outside the cabin was of wood; we burned wood in the fires, pine in the kitchen stove (more prone to sparking) and birch in the corner *peis* in the *stue*. It felt good to be living in wood, and these long dry bright days and all this wood.

In May the spring arrives a surprise with no obvious preparation. She's just very suddenly there, taking her place in the snow. And she's short, the spring, very short, and moves quickly. No sooner have the *lavskrike* pairs gathered the old man's black straggly beard for their nests, no sooner have we marvelled at the pasque flowers growing wild, and the tiny pale flowers of the *tyttebaer* and the *blåbaer* that almost look like berries from the start, no sooner have we noticed the bright pink bells of the ling, and watched the birches visibly leafing, the road verges and fields and *kves* all greening, greening so green in the warmth after the melt, no sooner all this than June arrives blazing with summer and there's willow fluff flying about and meadow cranesbill and cow parsley and the chickweed wintergreen speckles a universe of stars on the forest floor. Fields are bronzing with tiny fine docks and yellowing with buttercups and globe flowers and ladies' fingers, and that so fine plantain that has small white almost furry heads; everything bursting out at the same moment, within hours the landscape transforms into a mass of wavering colour and the nights get light instead of dark and there's a silver sliver of a moon just visible in the white night sky.

So these endless days we walk and we talk and A. works in the forest creating us a place in the trees to share with the ants and the elk and perhaps a red squirrel, a røyskatt, a badger, some burying voles. And we visit the still of little wooden churches and absorb the smell of the tar in the sun and the peace. In the evenings we listen to Vespers, we read by the fire in the stue, A. ploughing on with Thomas Mann and me, mostly old classics, re-reading things that keep gathering new importances as the years go by.

That's the *Dovrefjell* over there, with the snow on, straight ahead, as we're leaving the Oppdal *kjyrkje*.* The flag is set at half mast for there will be a funeral today. There's the grave, dug clean and waiting, the new-turned earth yet warm.

What a place to find eternal peace, she says to the dead person whose coffin is unloading from the back of the plain black car.

Would you mind so much if I shared your space? she asks, quietly. Only I saw you and I thought if I could just climb in there beside you, carefully, discreetly, is that alright? There, I'm not taking up much room, she says. See, I'm already cold, almost as cold as you.

Cold company, we can keep each other cold company, by the snow on the *Dovrefjell*, by the wild dark forest that wraps itself around us, by the little turf-roofed *lafthus* with their crumbling dry-stone chimneys, by the brown and white cattle who wander aimless and contented; by all of that, by God; it's good to know all of that's out there beside us, around us, isn't it, isn't it?

Come now, you hold onto me and we can cross this gorge, this deep cleft sliced in the mountain by some giant hand.

See the sun is no longer so high, see how the midnight moon is as close and as round and as big, how it casts its strange light on the green river that rushes out from under the glacier, see how it sprawls uneven shadows on the Viking mounds, on the burial grounds with their half-burnt bones.

Shall we go there, to the old grave lands?

Gud signe minnet

We can leave this earth-place any time we choose, depart from where they've placed us, placed us so carefully with nice carved stones and soft bright flowers, placed us among their kind whispered prayers.

Over døden skinner

Alle gode minner

We can leave this earth-place when we're ready, when the time is right, we can go, we can travel.

Elsket og savnet

Högt elska, sårt sakna

So come now, let us leave our earthy grave and go on to a different place. Hold my hand, you keep on holding my hand, dead friend I never knew in this life, and I'll say to you

Takk for alt

Hvil I fred.

We can be loved, now we are dead.

*Spellings for the word 'church' differ in Norway according to region and local dialect.

'Cleaning the Herring' won Dunbar's Wee Festival of Words short fiction competition 2013 and was published in their *Harbour* Anthology in support of RNLI. 'Picnicking with my Father' won the Lit & Phil's Ghost Stories competition and appeared in K. Fitzgerald, ed., (2013) *Root: New Stories from North East Writers*, Iron Press. 'Grandpa's Sweets' was written in an Innovative Fiction class at Edinburgh University and is dedicated to the late Helen Lamb (1956–2017). 'The Lilliput' was written in Jackie Kay's Memoir class at Newcastle University, was published in NCLA's *Alliterati magazine*, read at Storyshop at the Edinburgh International Book Festival 2013 and is dedicated with grateful thanks to Jackie Kay and Peggy Hughes. An academic version of 'The Shoes' was published in in A C Sparkes, ed., *Auto/Biography Yearbook* 2008. An earlier version of 'I'll Bloody Paris You' was used in Tees Valley Arts' 2018 campaign for libraries. An earlier version of 'Runaways' was commended in a Leaf Books Memoir competition and appeared in their anthology *Foresight with Hindsight*. 'Trapezium' began its life in an NCLA workshop with Sean O'Brien and was first published in *Inkapture* 2012. 'Help Yourself' was first published in *Radgepacket-on-line, Industrial strength fiction from Newcastle*. 'The Marriage' was published in *Cadenza* 18 (2008). It was written under the tutorship of Caron Freeborn at the Open University and has a special place in my heart—it was only the second story I wrote (the first was rubbish and was rightly savaged by Gordon Burn when I too quickly and too proudly showed it to him). 'Coconut Oil for Frying' was written in Howick Hall Gardens and was included in National Flash Fiction Day 2015's *Flash Flood*. 'Dolores and the Slick Men' was inspired by an image produced by student designer @ OrnamentalConifer, was originally commissioned by Amina Marix Evans for a charity event for *Borderline Books*, was read at the Edinburgh International Festival Fringe in further support of charities RNLI and Scottish Women's Aid, won Coastword's Short Story competition and was published in their anthology *Speak*. 'Jennifer and Nicola' first appeared in the on-line publication *Matchbook* and was anthologised by Laura Degnan of Writers' Block North East in her *Very Short Stories by Emerging Writers*. 'what are you like' took shape during a workshop with Iron Press's Pete Mortimer and an earlier version was originally part of a much longer piece 'The Purple' published in the Iron/Red Squirrel Press anthology *Short Not Sweet* (eds. Peter Mortimer and Sheila Wakefield). 'The Flesh Musketeers' was inspired by an image produced by Mike Michael. 'The Memory Box' was first published in *New Writing Scotland* 33 (eds. Gerry Cambridge and Diana Hendry). 'Skeleton in the Cupboard' was drafted in a workshop at NCLA on the work of Maurice Blanchot led by Lars Iyer. 'That Damned Old Cart Shed' began its life in an NCLA workshop with Bill Herbert and was read at the *Phantoms at the Phil* in 2018. 'Waiting' was first published in the inaugural issue of *Dactyl* and it was written for the late Ros Minsky. 'The Hole' was long listed for the Bath Flash Fiction Award 2018. 'A Brief Biography' first appeared in *New Writing Scotland* 31 (eds. Carl MacDougall and Zoe Strachan). 'Harry's Camellia' began its life in an NCLA Spring School in a workshop led by David Almond.

Some of the stories were written during extended summers in Norway and are dedicated with grateful thanks for friendship, hospitality, and so much more, to Thomas and Bjørg Dalene; Pål and Gerd Isum; Annette Giertsen and Raúl da Cunha; Leslie Bødtker; Louise and John Bødtker Downey; and Ruth and Eric Sejersted Bødtker; and Elisabeth Walter. Extra special *takk for alt* goes to Pål Audun Midtskog whose unbounded generosity restores the soul. Thanks for warm hospitality in Belgium, Benoît Fondu and Els Claes.

This little book began its life in 2015 when New Writing North deemed my stories worthy of a Northern Writer's Award and organized expert mentoring from Carys Davies. NWN has consistently supported me since 2011 when I began to take myself seriously as a writer. In 2017 they picked my debut novel *The Confession of Stella Moon* for their Read Regional Campaign.

Many people have helped at every stage of this book. I am immensely grateful to them all. My partner, Andrew Sclater, with his editor's eye and poet's ear, has given unflinching criticism, editorial help, and much much more. Jackie Kay was my creative writing tutor at NCLA and has been a continual sprinkler of magic dust ever since. My family—Poppy and Nick, Nico and Foxie, Trey and Abi, Chloe and Sophia, and Maddy and Barney; my besties Lin and Glyn, and Bula, Claire, Bethan, Simone and Caro; all my writing friends but most especially Angela Jackson, and Jacky and Victoria; the teams at Newcastle Noir, and NorthEastNoir, Edinburgh City of Literature, and the Scottish Book Trust, and The Literary Consultancy in London; my psychotherapist Jan; my trusty agent Jenny Brown—they've all been there for me and have helped me immeasurably on my writing journey. The late Helen Lamb was a friend and an inspiring teacher and she is greatly missed. Derek at *Boombarbers* is a genius with scissors. Contemporary writers breaking new ground who consistently inspire: Patti Smith, Ali Smith, AL Kennedy, Janice Galloway. Editor and Publisher Sheila Wakefield knows the best way to go about doing most things and it's been a real pleasure working with her and editor Colin Will.

I'm so grateful to all the reviewers and book bloggers who shouted out for my debut novel. I hope they'll be similarly enthused about this short story collection. Special thanks to Kelly Lacey @LoveBooksGroup.

Finally, huge thanks to my son Nicolai Sclater (aka Ornamental Conifer) for the cover artwork, and to my friend Gerry Cambridge for book design. I think you'll agree that together they've created a very beautiful object and I won't mind a bit if people judge this particular book by its cover.

Shelley Day, Vollsdammen, Norway, July 2018.

A NOTE ON THE TYPES

This collection is set in Joanna Nova and Joanna Nova Sans, contemporary updates on the Eric Gill classic typeface Joanna. The updated versions feature a greatly extended set of weights and styles, and add a sans serif which was not available in Gill's original.

*

Shelley Day was named as an Edinburgh UNESCO City of Literature 'emerging writer' in 2013 and has since appeared at numerous literary festivals. Her debut novel *The Confession of Stella Moon* (Saraband, 2016) won the Andrea Badenoch Prize and was shortlisted for the Dundee International Book Prize. In 2015 she won a Northern Writer's Award to support this debut short story collection.